I fell bac_____ ..___._.vu...or door.

I had nothing to defend myself with, no spritzer, no bag. Shoes. I pulled off my heels, one in each hand. I heard the elevator car settle in behind me. Stephan lunged for me. I shrank back from his grasp, remembered the shoe in my own hand and swung for his head.

He was not getting me back.

Stephan ducked the swing. The elevator dinged. I swung with my left, he caught it, dragged me to him.

"Ashley, stop!"

The elevator door began sliding open. I looked over his shoulder. The onlookers had disappeared from the hall. That warm presence slid along the inside of my skull, fumbling, trying to take over. I yanked wildly at my arm.

"Ashley, it's okay."
"No, it's not!"

I glanced behind me, glimpsed what looked like ship's officers' uniforms in the car. I froze. No one could know. No one ever.

Praise for Tonya Macalino's
SPECTRE OF INTENTION

Amazon Reader Reviews:

"'Spectre of Intention' is a cross-genre triumph. Tonya Macalino spins a story webbed with threads of romance, science fiction, mystery and thrill—all cocooned into one gripping ride."

"Both the read and the ride are fast, furiously addictive, and fantastically executed. Overall, a damn fine read!"

"If you like reading character-driven fiction with a strong protagonist and a deft narrative style that never interferes with an old-fashioned ripping good yarn, then Spectre of Intention should be your next read."

"Tonya Macalino – remember this name. You'll be seeing a lot of it in the years to come."

"The villains are bad, the heroes are good, and yet they all manage to rise above stereotypes and cardboard cutouts to become real people with real motivations that the reader can truly care about. All in all, a fabulous first novel, and one that I'm sure will build a fanbase eager for more of Macalino's work."

"I highly recommend it for anyone who likes their romance with a lot of mystery, history, sci fi and paranormal aspects all rolled into one!"

Media Reviews:

"Spectre of Intention had me from the beginning... I couldn't read it fast enough!!... I look forward to reading more from Tonya Macalino! I recommend this book to others and purchase it as a gift. Put it on your TBR list!!"

- Keeping Up With The Rheinlanders

"Spectre of Intention is a fantastic read . . . a novel that puts a very sci-fi spin on what initially seems to be a traditional caper, but quickly becomes something more....This is a very dark, very edgy, very creepy story, but there are some moments of romance and humour. It's a very tense read, and one that almost demands your full attention, so the brief mood changes are definitely welcome. Fast-paced, with well-written dialogue, and a mystery that teases you from chapter to chapter, this was definitely a fun read."

- Bibrary Book Lust

"The author skillfully winds us in future-tech woven with psi-abilities and explores every person's right to privacy. Action-packed, *Spectre of Intention* is ripe with physical vocabulary designed to keep you attuned to Kaitlin's fear and longing. An intelligent, well-researched scifi is always good to find, and I learned a ton about space elevators. The human story in this book balances the physical science for the technically impaired, mixed in with spicy scenes of passion between the heroine and Cam Glaswell (fans self)."

- Kelly McCrady, author of The Empire's Edge

"Tonya Macalino is definitely a writer to watch! SPECTRE OF INTENTION is a fresh, intriguing novel with a captivating heroine."

- Donna Fletcher Crow, author of A Very Private Grave

Love free books?

Receive free books and exclusive content
written just for members of the Reader Group.
Download special book launch party gifts.

Join the
TONYA MACALINO READER GROUP
at
www.TonyaMacalino.com

SPECTRE
OF
INTENTION

TONYA MACALINO

CRYSTAL
MOSAIC
BOOKS

This is a work of fiction. All of the characters, organizations, and events portrayed in this novel are either products of the author's imagination or are used fictitiously, and any resemblance to actual persons, living or dead, business establishments or events is entirely coincidental.

SPECTRE OF INTENTION

For information, address Crystal Mosaic Books, PO Box 1276 Hillsboro, OR 97123

ISBN: 978-0-9836303-0-2

Printed in the United States of America

For my parents,
For whom no dream
Was ever too big.

ACKNOWLEDGEMENTS

I would like to thank my husband Ray for slugging through oh so many manuscripts during his very precious spare time. And my kids for listening to Mommy go on and on about the latest developments in space elevator technology—as though that were the most fascinating subject in the world.

To my brother, Jack, for snickering at all my technical mistakes and my sister, Trixy, for tactfully pointing out the psychological and physiological inconsistencies.

I would also like to give a nod to my critique group: Rob Richards, Margaret Hammitt-McDonald, Tom Cutts, and Teri Watanabe. Thanks for taking me in and challenging my brain!

For their generosity, kindness, and support through the publication process, I would acknowledge John Vincent and Lisa Holmes. Thanks again.

And last, but absolutely not least, my own personal cheerleader, Teri Watanabe, for endless encouragement when a certain someone got discouraged, for retrieving untold numbers of errant prepositions and pronouns, and for helping decode the back end of publishing.

My love to you all.

SPECTRE
OF
INTENTION

For Mysti —
Here's to that first
brave, blind step!

1

Who was it who ran away like this?

Lady Liberty never said, "Give me your social outcasts, your criminals, your bored, your adrenaline junkies." But that was because she was scripted with poetry, colored with hope.

So, who was it *really* who ran away like this?

I had been all those things Lady Liberty never said she collected, but would I have ever considered this?

The gray ribbon dangled from the center of a perfect blue sky; its slender length held up by nothing, having no beginning, only an ending here on the gleaming white platform where I stood. I tilted my head back, the infinitesimal sway of the great cruise ship leaving me floating, feeling as though I could reach up into that sky and grasp hold of that ribbon, as though I could give in to its seductive song: *Come away, come away with me. Leave this all behind and begin again. This time it will be right. This time it will be real. No more lies, just a pure, new beginning.*

My hand floated up, but I lowered it back to the textured blue-gray silk of my skirt, dried the sweat from my palm. I had tried that before, the running. As desperate as I had been, as terrified as I was now, I didn't think that would have driven me here.

Pioneer's Port.

No, I definitely didn't have the stuff of a pioneer. To be frozen, canned, raised up this elevator ribbon to the glittering emptiness of space, packaged neatly in a voyager, and shot off toward a promising-looking speck of light whose only name was a meaningless jumble of numbers and letters.

I felt the familiar pull, warm and gentle behind me, long before his large hand settled on my shoulder.

"Kaitlin." My boss and mentor, Jessie Broadbent, squeezed my shoulder.

I sighed and smiled, comforted despite myself.

He kept his deep, rich voice low. "We've gotten this far. Everything's going to be fine."

"Five years isn't so long ago, and this isn't some playboy's mansion or a corporate fortress with a little hole that needs patching." I turned to face him, and his hand slid away across the back of my suit jacket. "This is international security, a long-term, high-profile contract. They're going to look. They're going to find out."

A smile creased Jessie's tanned, outdoorsman face, framing his bright green eyes with the beginnings of crow's feet. "If they were going to say something, they would have done it by now. We won this contract thanks to your sales expertise. No more cold feet. Kaitlin Osgood doesn't get cold feet."

No, but Ashley Porter sure as hell did. Especially when my signature at the bottom of that contract could be the last nail they needed for my coffin...if they knew. I took a deep breath, slid Ashley Porter back into her windowed closet where she was allowed to look out at the life we lived, but where her commentary would remain—after all these years—largely silenced. As my spine straightened and the worry slid from my face, Kaitlin settled back into place. I saw the satisfaction in Jessie's eyes.

I inclined my head. "Shall we go sign the contracts, Mr. Broadbent?"

Jessie gestured for me to lead the way. Always the gentleman.

◆

The operations side of the ship gave the impression of a neatly labeled rat maze, winding in on itself and tricking you from reaching your goal by means of endless sameness. Little cash had been put into softening the laboratory look of the halls and offices with their sharp right angles, shiny institutional flooring, and blinding white walls. More than abovedeck I itched for the sunglasses I'd left in my cabin.

By the time we reached conference room 5-F, I knew that if gremlins came along and removed all the small block-lettered signs along the hallway, Jessie and I would never find our way out again. Well, Jessie might, but by this point I was thoroughly turned around. The narrow meeting room we had been assigned even had laboratory-style mirrored observation windows down either side. Creepy. I glanced back at Jessie, but his hero mode had already been replaced with hardened security professional. I jerked Kaitlin over me a little tighter as he reached past me and opened the door.

White laminate conference table; cushionless, velcro-to-your-nylons blue upholstery on the chairs. Better than stainless steel with floor drains, I guessed.

A chair scraped as we entered the room: the don of the Pioneer Port Authority, William Nye. His perfectly tailored suit and elegantly sculpted white hair matched the steady, focused push I felt radiating off him. Not a cold or fiery push of negative intent, but that relentless forward energy that said he was already half way through this meeting and onto his next billion-dollar decision.

Seated to his right, J.C. Brands, Port Operations Manager, looked up at William. He seemed to consider rising as well, then sent us a vague smile and returned to reading whatever was on his workpad. No negative intent there either, just the swirl of warm thrill and frustrated fire of a man focused on untangling the kind of problems he loved. I smiled at J.C.'s thinning pate and strode across the room to shake William's hand.

"Mr. Nye, I would like to introduce my boss and CEO of Countermeasures International, Jessie Broadbent. Jessie, Mr. William Nye."

"Will, please," Mr. Nye corrected as I stepped aside so the two men could shake hands. "Please have a seat. Mr. Glaswell, our Director of Port Security, will join us in a moment."

Jessie looked to me. I smiled and gave a small shake of my head, got an I-told-you-so look in return. No, if the calling out was going to come, it was going to come from the man who belonged in the empty chair next to J.C. So that's where I sat, directly in front of that empty chair.

And hoped. Hoped that it wouldn't be him. Anybody but him.

The silence stretched. Logistically, it should have been my role to start up the conversation. My mind stayed stubbornly blank.

So, Will, with his impeccable manners, set up the play. "I'm counting on you and your team to test my staff during your stay. We expect to take our first prospective clients aboard in six months. Any of the restaurants, fitness facilities, hotel staff, spa, recreation—it's all free while you're here, if you fill out the comment screen at the end of each day."

Spa. If I survived this meeting, I was headed straight over.

"Thank you, Will. I'll be sure to inform the rest of my team of your generous offer," Jessie replied.

"I'm serious about this. I expect four-star service out of my people and there's only one way to find out if they are going to give it."

"Understood, sir."

Nope. Jessie was not going to pick up that ball for me. I was definitely going to have to run with it myself.

"So, Will—"

The door popped behind me. I nearly popped out of my seat. I did end up coming up out of my chair, just to see, just to finally know what was coming at me. As I turned, it grabbed me—a jerk of intention directed so forcefully at me personally that it had me hanging onto the back of my chair for balance. Bright blue eyes, shimmering with vitality. That sharp pull tightened, our first meeting in the flesh, the recognition in his fresh, vivid face, reflecting back the curiosity I knew he saw in mine. For a year we had worked together only as voices—a fast, well-matched rhythm, a pair of clever minds. For a year, I had known him without knowing him. Now here he was with the power to destroy my life.

He shifted the stack of workpads onto one arm to push back a short sweep of sandy, sun-bleached hair.

The movement broke the moment.

His intention shifted abruptly into a snarl of hot and cold, push and pull. Completely unreadable. *Oh, shit.*

Inside my brain, Ashley slammed open the closet door, "The perfect hair, the perfect blue dress shirt with the perfect tie. Don't trust this guy. Get away! Get the fucking hell away!" Kaitlin grabbed that ragged old me and shoved her back inside, held the door closed against her hysteria. Kaitlin thought the man in that perfect blue shirt was the most beautiful, the most dangerous thing she had ever seen.

I watched Camden Glaswell circle the sharp corners of the table followed by his two lieutenants. In my business, in my past, I had known a myriad of different types of law enforcement professionals. Protect and serve. Some embraced different faces of the protector: the tough guy; the righteous soldier...or the unfortunate bureaucrat with a badge. For others it was the chance to play war games. Camden Glaswell came to it to help. Pure and simple. That much was in his face. That much made me want to let Ashley take the helm and run. But more important was what made Kaitlin nervous: the way his easy smile—as it crept up to fill those all too intelligent eyes—bore no trace of his disjointed emotional focus.

None of that stopped me from reaching out to take his offered hand, from letting that tingle of contact creep slowly up my arm.

"Nice to finally meet you, Cam."

"How was the trip, Kaitlin? Any problems getting your sea legs?"

He looked so concerned; I smiled just to reassure him. "Barely noticeable."

God, what were those eyes trying to see? I forced myself to relax under his scrutiny.

Finally, Cam released me to shake Jessie's hand. "And the trip, Mr. Broadbent?"

"It was a smooth ride. Thank you, Mr. Glaswell."

On that, I had to shoot Jessie a wry grin. A four-hour flight from Miami to Ecuador, a quick three-hour hop over to the Enchanted Islands, followed by a twelve-hour boat ride from the Galapagos to this unknown point in the Pacific. It would probably be exactly that many days more until my brain realigned with my body. Jessie was, of course, fine.

As Cam passed out the workpads with the contracts, I settled back into my chair. So, I couldn't read him. Then time to try the lieutenants. I introduced myself to each of them to give me the excuse to focus on them directly. The first woman was dark, maybe part African, part Hispanic. Ms. Davina Soto, Operations Security. Everything coming off of her said we were not her pick to receive the contract. Her negativity focused more on Cam and Will with a little left over for Jessie and me. And then came the grinning redhead: Mr. Arlen McEnnis, Hospitality Security. Who was pretty much exclusively thinking about nailing me against the wall.

Okay, next!

I pulled the contract verification cards from my shoulder bag and handed one to Jessie. He looked at me for confirmation, but I could only shrug my eyebrows. I wanted to be reassured. Davina and Arlen seemed to have no knowledge. Will and J.C. didn't seem to know. I couldn't believe that Cam would have kept that kind of information from his boss or the managers he'd brought with him to the face-off. I should have been reassured...but alone, in my self-imposed exile, I just couldn't read intentions like I used to. I couldn't see what people wanted to do. I could only guess by feel—and that would always leave so much room for misunderstanding.

Time to take the leap.

Jessie and I passed the cards our lawyer had prepared for us over the workpad's reader. After a moment, the card flashed green with confirmation that no unapproved changes had been detected. I navigated through the signature screens, then laid my hand over the screen just as Will, Jessie, and Cam did.

Bio-signature one confirmed.
Raise pad for bio-signature two.

I aligned the marks on the screen with my eyes.

Bio-signature two confirmed.
Signed contract being transmitted.

Transmission complete.
Receipt of contract confirmed by:
Miller, Kohlson, and Associates.
3:00 p.m. EDT
May 13, 2048

It was done.

Nobody was pulling out badges. Or guns. Or handcuffs.

I probed out across the table. Cam's frenetic, unintelligible emotional state remained unchanged.

Could I really have gotten away with it?

Ashley wasn't buying it. In any other moment, the force of her distrust could have cracked that closet door, set her free. In any other moment. In this moment, Kaitlin struggled to keep a very unprofessional foolish grin off my face.

I glanced over at Jessie, the adrenaline of relief pounding through me so hard, I had to tuck my hands beneath the table. Jessie rose and Mr. Nye got to his feet as well. The two men shook hands vigorously. I dried my cold palms as Cam pushed up from his chair. Our turn. As his hand caught mine, he gave a little pull, drawing me forward over the table.

Beneath the congratulations of the other men, he murmured, "Are you alright, Kaitlin?"

Even Kaitlin couldn't suppress a slight blush at that. Was it that obvious? With my hidden little ability, I'd long ago become damn good at hiding my reactions to the things I shouldn't know. Cam gave my hand a little rub. I looked down.

Ah, the cold hands, I realized.

"I'm fine. Just tired." I looked up into all that concern. "Thank you for all your help through this. Now I guess we'll find out how well you hold up during deployment. If we are both still alive, I'll buy you a beer on November 1st."

He laughed at that. "So, you're trying to get out of the one you said you'd buy me at the end of the contracts."

I shot him a sly grin and pulled my hand free.

I exchanged nods with J.C. and the lieutenants, handshakes with Mr. Nye. I turned to pack our legal confirmation cards away when Mr. Nye cleared his throat.

"Camden here feels that your company has the best mastery of the kind of security technology this port requires. And I trust him."

I heard a "but" coming and straightened, turning. Ashley tensed.

Mr. Nye gave Jessie, then me a pointed stare.

Then it came.

"But, I believe in learning from history's mistakes. As my people know, I see this port as the launching point for pioneers, pilgrims looking for better lives and new beginnings. Those original Pilgrims, the ones that first sailed for America, they trusted, too."

Will settled his briefcase on the table top like a podium. Ashley had a death grip on my bag's handle that I couldn't release. Trust, he kept saying. Where was he going with this?

"The Pilgrims put their lives and their fortunes in the hands of Captain Reynolds and the crew of the Speedwell. Have you heard of the Speedwell?"

I shook my head, saw Jessie nod. Ashley had one eye on the door. As if there were somewhere to run, out here in the middle of the Pacific. Kaitlin double-checked the expression of polite interest on my face, made sure it matched the rest of the room's occupants. I tried to feed from the press of their boredom and suspended impatience, but an underlying frisson of discomfort skittered across my arm from the other side of the table...Arlen, maybe Davina. Not the time to look. Not when Will had decided to focus his speech directly on me now.

"Two ships were to have sailed to the New World, Miss Osgood. The Mayflower and the Speedwell. But you rarely hear of the Speedwell. That's because this Captain Reynolds used their trust to commit sabotage. He had the boat refitted with masts that were too tall, putting too much torque on the hull. The pressure caused gaps between the planks and the ship began to take on water. Our clever Captain Reynolds purposely put the Pilgrims out one ship, a quarter of their people, and likely a good bit of critical cargo as well. All to save himself a long, treacherous voyage and to placate the officials of a treacherous Dutch government."

Trust. Treacherous. Betrayal. Is that what he thought? I never hid Ashley to betray anyone. Far, far from it. Will smiled as he lifted his briefcase from the table and nudged his chair back out of the way.

"Human trust is fallible, and I don't want my team caught second-guessing each other, waiting to become the next elevator to succumb to a terrorist attack from within. I want hope to be the focus here, not fear. So, before this ship takes on a single passenger, I will expect everyone affiliated with this project to be thoroughly screened by this intention detection technology of yours with its statistically impossible two percent error rate. Myself and yourselves included. There will be no one exempt. There will be no Captain Reynolds here."

"Yes, sir," I nodded, and Jessie echoed me.

Then Jessie and I turned and slipped out the door.

We walked in silence through the length of the rat's maze.

We passed through the simple security between operations and hospitality.

We made it twenty feet down the plush carpeted hall to the elevator.

I burst into hysterical laughter.

"Oh, my god, he had me there at the end. He really had me. God, I think I'm going to faint."

Jessie shook his head but took my arm just in case.

"No faith. Come on, Osgood. Time to go do a little celebrating."

Celebrating. Kaitlin wanted to throw confetti at the stars. But deep in the corner of her darkness, Ashley whispered about the inevitable sunrise, the dawn that would bring this long masquerade to an end.

And I chose to ignore her.

2

"Hey, my favorite pair of suits!"

Gerard swung us into the ship's tiny sports pub with a gigantic pint of beer in his hand. And immediately began to chug down what appeared to be a good strong Guinness for long enough that I started holding my breath, wondering how much longer he could possibly keep going. He slammed down the empty glass next to Paula's workpad. She jumped, and Gerard tossed back his head in laughter.

"To our first billion!"

Jessie lifted the brimming glass Gerard handed him. "To our first billion." He took a short drag from beneath the foam.

Gerard slapped a hand to his own chest in melodramatic disappointment.

"Come on, man, if I'm gonna keep your pace, you're gonna have to buy me a replacement. Step this way to the buffet, my friend."

I laughed, still too giddy to settle in for a long-overdue meal. Gerard, lean and pretty-faced, dragged his bulkier partner over to a table loaded with bar food and shouted for another Guiness. I leaned against the dark buttery wood of the table where Paula tapped furiously away at her screen in the dim light and watched the owners of Countermeasures International fall backwards in time through the portal of a beer glass.

I couldn't really follow their friendship. Jessie was serious and steady, brilliant and ruthless, and a hero to the core of his gold heart. Gerard was the guy who ends up dead by the middle of the military buddy movie—the reckless "kid" full of joie de vivre but missing the real reasons for being here. If at that critical moment five years ago, I had reached out to Gerard instead of Jessie, I would be pregnant and back on the street by now. Fortunately, I was better at reading people than your average refugee.

Jessie should have bored Gerard; Gerard should have tested the strength of Jessie's last nerve. Instead, they seemed to balance each other. They divided tasks naturally between their strengths and weaknesses. I opened doors; they wordlessly took control of buildings. They had served in the Army together; they took what they had learned there, kept right on fighting. And now I was a part of it.

"Would you stop that?"

I laughed down at Paula. "What?"

"If Gerard sees you looking over there with all that hero-worship in your eyes, he's going to walk over here and try to find a way to get laid and I'm going to have to sit through it."

Whoops, time to put Ashley back away.

"Which is precisely why I don't let him within ten feet of me. He can go buy himself a blow-up doll if he's that horny." Not a very Kaitlin thing to say, or maybe it was. Anyway, time to change the subject. I pushed at Paula's pad. "What are you working on? Why aren't you over there getting drunk?"

Paula ruffled her sleek mahogany hair, then tried to rub the life back into her petite, pale face.

"I was flipping through the micro-expressions database and came up with an idea I want to try."

"Let me see." I reached for the workpad and suddenly Jessie was right in front of us. He pushed the pad back to Paula.

"Not for you."

Ignoring the sting of that parental wrist slap took the focus of every cell in my body, but Kaitlin didn't take things like that personally. She didn't wince with hurt. She just smiled and shook her hair back. Jessie stared me down, making sure his point had been taken. With a reinforcing tap on the table, he turned away and returned to Gerard and his dreams of what to do with his share of the billion. I glanced back at Paula, but she wouldn't meet my gaze.

With a sigh, I pushed off the table and wandered toward the bar and the man doomed to wait on our tiny celebration. Above his head, flashes of a hockey game shared space with baseball, basketball, and soccer.

"Champagne for the lady?"

With the readiness of a well-trained host, the bartender held the glass out for me. I smiled and thanked him, turned back toward the room, only then realizing that left me standing with a glass of champagne in my hand. I didn't need to look to feel the yank of concern from Jessie. I gazed down at the golden liquid effervescing inches from my lips. One little sip; how bad could it be? Kaitlin would drink champagne to celebrate a moment like this.

I raised the glass to my lips.

Just one little sip.

Wine splashed over my tongue, tart and tingly, freeing. Freeing, granting Ashley full control of my brain and body. She wanted it all. She wanted it NOW.

No.

I breathed through it, willed Kaitlin back in control. Kaitlin set that glass back down. Kaitlin walked away from that bar. Kaitlin met the reproach in Jessie's eyes with indifference.

"I think I'm more exhausted than I thought. I'm going to head up for a hot bath and some room service. I'll see you boys and girls in the morning."

Kaitlin spared Paula a nod, then walked away.

◆

I got myself to the elevator. I reached for the ninth floor button but met with resistance. I wasn't ready yet to be caged up in my room. By god, I'd just signed a billion-dollar contract, a contract I'd spearheaded! My finger hovered over the button for the entertainment deck, then the deck advertising a park; passed the pools and the spa; settled on a set of decks that held "observation decks." I chose one at random and settled back for the ride.

The alcohol-lust still churned in my gut, but my mind was so full, it was easy to find something else to distract me.

Cam.

He was so different from what I'd expected. I'd looked forward to meeting him. Our working relationship had been filled with the light, short banter that made the day go faster—simple fun. So, I'd expected, apparently foolishly, more of the same once I came onboard. But Cam in person, god, those eyes. And that mind, there was nothing simple about that mind.

Even if he knew nothing...

I caught myself tapping out my nerves on the railing.

Even if he knew nothing, I was in trouble in more ways than one.

The elevator door opened, and I laughed to myself.

I stepped out into another hallway. This one was old-fashioned with real wood wainscoting on the walls, a richly patterned velvet-style wallpaper on the upper half of the walls. The fixtures were ornate brass, the floors, wood with an embedded carpet runner down the center. I followed the signs to the observation deck.

Brocade wing-back chairs studded the rear of the room. I passed them by, running my fingers along the ridges of the cool, satiny fabric. I followed a rail down to the floor-to-ceiling window that should have overlooked the elevator launch pad. But hours had bled into one another and it was dark now. The deck lights which, in just a couple months would illuminate the ribbon of nanotubes and its elevator climber, waited dormant for the ship's less utilitarian occupancy.

So, I was left looking out at blackness, most of the stars flooded out by the boat's safety lights. The sliver of moon served as the primary reminder of the heavens this vessel promised. I looked down. At the base of the window, in heavy gold script lay the title of the room: The Dream.

I glanced around the walls of the observation deck and realized that I had missed the artwork, images from a dozen ancient cultures framed in gold and richly stained woods. Curious, I strode to the first.

Done in the stylistic strokes of old Chinese art, the image depicted a thinly bearded man in the heavy layers of his finery sitting atop a floating chair, one hand raised to the moon, a flock of cranes sailing by on a lazy breeze. I read the placard next to the picture.

"According to legend, **Wan Hu,** a minor official of the Ming dynasty, circa mid-1500s, attempted to become the first pioneer of space travel. Seating himself upon a chair mounted with forty-seven rockets, he gave the command and his forty-seven servants lit one fuse each. There followed a great billow of smoke and a terrible rumble. When the air had cleared, both chair and pioneer were gone.

A crater on the far side of the moon now bears his name."

I laughed—a little too loudly for such an empty space. So that's who did it. It wasn't the wildly desperate or the wildly bored. It was the abject lunatics.

I wandered down the row, saw images from an ancient Persian epic, another throne pointed toward the heavens, this time propelled by great clawed eagles. The next portrait, a black and white of a five-thousand-year-old seal from Babylonia, the raised edges nearly erased by time, but there it was again, the mind of man reaching for the moon and stars, this time forgoing the throne, being borne aloft by a magnificent bird.

I stopped when I had come full circle, looked up again at the shine of that perfect crescent hanging in the sky. I laid my hand on the window, over that silvery light. The Dream. It should have been impossible, but our ancestors kept trying, kept fighting and dying over a chance to realize that dream, to become a part of the magic of the heavens. Sometimes my own simpler dream felt that impossible. Sometimes I felt like an abject lunatic for trying. But maybe, just maybe my fighting was done, too. Maybe I could stop looking over my shoulder and start looking forward.

Even as I thought that, a seeping warmth bloomed at the back of my head, my heart, my stomach.

Him.

Trying to take over.

I shook my head, shook out my limbs. The sensation fled. So pathetic. Out in the middle of the Pacific Ocean, the only part of my past here to haunt me...was me.

And only if I let it.

Out of the corner of my eye I saw the sweep of a flashlight in the dimly lit hall. How small an action to change the comfort of solitude into the chill of isolation. I reached into my bag and palmed a small spritzer of perfume, then turned my purposeful stride up the ramp. I could feel the hot anger coming toward me, knew it would hit me full on once the bearer of all that good will rounded the corner.

The guard and I saw each other at the same time. He lowered his flashlight and for a second, I thought I saw something I hadn't seen in a half a decade: the energy of his intention become corporeal. Ghosting ahead of his own body, a raging image of the man raised his transparent fist and took a swing at me.

I couldn't stop myself from dodging. His intention scrambled as he stared at me like I was crazy. The ghost image vanished. Probably never even there.

Abject lunatic was right.

I kept my face blank, kept walking right past him, listened for his footsteps behind me. Didn't hear them.

Caucasian male; six-foot one; two hundred pounds; short wavy black hair; large brown eyes; pronounced cheek bones; heavy on the stubble potential; large hands with cornered thumbs; size 14 shoe, slight turn out on right foot.

When it came time to vet the staff, that guy was going on a growing list of people who hated me. He'd be on the first boat back to shore.

Tough shit.

I hit the elevator. The perfume didn't slide back into my bag until I saw the doors close over the vacant, antique hallway.

◆

I breathed out the last of my adrenaline against the evacuation instructions on the back of my cabin door. I reached over my left shoulder and secured the door bolt. Sometimes I wondered if knowing what I knew was entirely fair. Maybe the guard was just pissed that some dumb blonde had set off the alarm and interrupted his poker game. That didn't make him a sociopath. Of course, wanting to beat her face in over it kind of did.

If what I'd seen had been a real incarnation of his intent in the first place.

With a sigh, I tossed my bag in the middle of the bed's bronze coverlet, checked the wall pad for any messages. Cam had scheduled our first meeting for ten o'clock the next morning. I chuckled. How thoughtful of him to plan some time for hangover recovery.

I kicked off my heels. My hamstrings screamed even as my soles sighed down into the soothing softness of the white carpet. I flung my jacket over my bag and stretched out the rest of my cramped body.

I wandered over to the mirrored closet facing my bed. Time to let Ashley out. I lowered my guard, lowered my body to the floor. Here was the street rat's longest con: Kaitlin Osgood, Senior VP, Sales and Project Management for Countermeasures International. Seeing my own face in the mirror no longer gave me a jolt. Jessie and I had taken away the street rat's kinky brown hair, replaced it with a stylish gold-blonde, shoulder-length swing.

We'd dyed the brown eyes a serious shade of blue-gray. Hours at the gym had peeled away the roundness of fast food; the simple passage of years had transitioned a soft child's face into the sculpted lines of a woman who knew exactly what she wanted but could still laugh about it.

Kaitlin Osgood.

Ashley reached out and touched the lines of Kaitlin's face, traced her hair with more than a bit of wonder. Who might I have become if I'd never met Jessie? Ashley tried to place an image of herself over the blonde executive in the mirror.

She wanted the gentle image of my mother, the nurse.

She could con anyone, but me.

I corrected her idyllic portrait:

Hard, sunken lines framing a hard mouth and yet harder eyes. Anger, suspicion, and the restlessness of addiction. Rough hair, rough skin with the perpetual pink stain of alcohol. A worn wardrobe that could never keep up with the weight gain.

She could con anyone, but me.

The wall pad behind me beeped. Ashley slid without protest back into her closet.

I rose from the floor, feeling long and light on my feet after spending that little moment without the mask. I touched the screen and Cam's face appeared. That was unusual. He was a voice-only kind of guy. I turned on the video from my end with a smile.

Surprise flashed over his face. I reached up to toy with my necklace and realized why. The lacy cream-colored camisole from my suit probably looked a whole lot like lingerie from the camera's perspective.

"Ah, am I calling too late?" he asked.

I laughed. "No, I just got to my room. What's on your mind?"

"Well, I just got out of my last meeting and I thought I'd see if you wanted to go celebrate."

This was a really dumb idea. I was so exhausted that I was seeing things and the man who probably knew too much wanted me to go play mental chess with him.

But god, those eyes.

"I'd love to. Give me about twenty minutes to wash the day off. Where do I meet you?"

"At the Parkside Café. See you in twenty."

He signed off with a victorious grin.

As I moved in the direction of the shower, I acknowledged that this wasn't going to be dinner between business associates. Ethical or not, I was being courted. And now I had to decide if I was ready to give Kaitlin a boyfriend.

3

I recognized, as I stepped out of the mirrored elevator, that my wardrobe choice indicated I'd already made up my mind. The flowing white summer dress with its chunks of silver sparkle along the neckline might have been a bit overdone on some women, but I'd long since learned Kaitlin could pull it off and still look classy. As for the actual state of my mind, I had forgotten in my distraction to check the ship's map and now walked confidently down the pale blue halls trimmed in birch bark, waiting patiently for any directional signage to appear so that I could adjust my course accordingly.

And if something didn't appear very soon, I was going to be very late.

Then suddenly the right side of the hall gave way to a wall of smoky glass. Over the open doors in the center hung the shingle "Parkside Café." I stepped into the dimly lit waiting area. A very bored, very young maitre d' looked up from his podium.

"Miss Osgood?"

I smiled and nodded.

The spectre of his intention stepped out from behind the podium, reached out to feel the skin of my naked arms. I stared as those ghostly hands moved over my flesh.

"Miss Osgood, this way please."

I jerked my head up. I should go. This shouldn't be happening. I shouldn't be seeing his intention. Especially not for something so trivial. I should get back to my room. I should call Jessie. Something...something was wrong with me.

The young man reached my side, reabsorbed his ghostly self, and took its place. In a formal gesture, he raised his elbow and I slipped my hand through. His spectral hand came to rest on my forearm, gently stroking as he told me the specials for the evening. I didn't hear a word, didn't feel a thing but the horrible pressure in my head.

The maitre d' led me through a narrow room with seating raised in tiers up the wall to overlook a lovely leafy park full of flowers and fairy lights. We stepped out the restaurant doors and into the steamy night air and the pressure in my head evaporated. My escort's intention faded slowly from view.

I took a deep breath; my eyes came to rest on Cam seated at one of the tables arrayed on a cobblestone patio at the edge of the wooded garden.

"Sir, your guest has arrived."

Cam set down his wine glass, unfolded his long frame from the chair. He, too, had changed: a light-weight white button-down shirt and a pair of khakis. So different from the perfect suit and tie of this afternoon.

"Thanks, Justin. I'll let you know when we're ready to order."

"Yes, sir."

Justin moved away. I heard the door close behind me. Like last time, that fascinated pull from Cam was sharp—and this time not one-sided. I stepped forward, close enough to smell the clean, earthy scent of his cologne. I wanted to lift my hand, touch one of the pearlescent buttons of his shirt, but that was so personal. I saw his hand twitch, stretch. Ashley whimpered quietly in the back of my mind. I smiled.

I looked up into those vivid blue eyes. "You are nothing like I expected."

A wry amusement twisted his mouth, lent extra shine to his eyes.

"Is that so? Over the course of a whole year you didn't look me up even once?"

I shook my head. "That would have been cheating. I was enjoying your mind too much to want to spoil it."

His hand did move then, up to toy with the chunk of metal decorating the shoulder strap of my dress. "And is your impression of me now utterly ruined?"

Yes, I wanted to say, *that carefree, platonic fun is now utterly ruined.* But I just laughed as the brush of his fingers sent a tingle down my arm that pooled distractingly in my fingertips. "You are so vivid, so...alive. Like something that could just go bounding off through those trees and vanish. Much too mysterious for the world of business suits."

Cam looked startled for a moment. Then he burst out laughing. "I thought all the good men of mystery wore business suits."

I turned toward my seat at the table. "Depends on what kind of mystery you're after, I suppose."

I reached for the back of my chair, but he beat me to it. My back brushed against his chest as he pulled the chair out. I had to catch myself from leaning into him, into all that hard warmth. I hurried to sit down.

He took his seat across from me. "Well, I did cheat. About four months into it, but I have to say you don't look anything at all like your old pictures."

Old pictures. So, we begin.

The pull didn't lessen, but unease shimmered through my stomach as that tangle rose up in him. I leaned forward, moved my pawn. "Old pictures. And which old pictures did you get hold of?"

Cam leaned forward as well, his laughing eyes turning crystal for a second. What I would have given to see the incarnation of his intention right then. But there was no pressure in the head, no momentary short of the senses. Just the two of us in the stillness of the moment, trying to see past the practiced polish of the façade.

And failing.

Cam picked up his menu, put it between us. I did the same. I could almost feel him fishing for a legitimate answer to that question, the pause went on so long.

"Just pictures from a conference. You were making a sales presentation, I believe. You had dark-framed glasses on and your hair pinned back and looked as intimidating as the Spanish Inquisition, but here you were on the phone with me making dumb jokes and laughing at mine with this voice that was as sexy as hell. So," he paused looking up over his menu at me, "cheating didn't do me a damn bit of good."

"Have you ever been a woman in her early twenties at a security conference?"

"I can't say as I have."

"But I think you can guess how very necessary that costume was to my career at the time."

"Even now? We're a bit far from the days of the women's rights movement."

I took a sip from my water, heard the door to the restaurant open punctually behind me, and quickly scanned the menu as I answered. "More the youth than the gender, but the gender was still a factor. Jessie calls it my Catholic school teacher costume. Spanish Inquisition. I'll have to tell him that."

"Have you had a chance to decide?" Justin asked.

Cam looked to me; I nodded at him to go ahead.

"I'll have the cedar-planked salmon with roasted vegetables."

I closed the menu and handed it to Justin.

"I'll take the chicken pot pie." I could already feel all that warm protein sliding into a stomach that had finally settled enough to consider such mundane matters.

"Anything to drink?"

"I'll stick with water, but I owe the gentleman a beer."

"Which he will be all too happy to accept. An IPA, please. And an order of the flatbread with caramelized pecans, blue cheese, and minced dates." He handed Justin his empty wine glass.

"I'll be right back with that, sir. Ma'am."

Justin disappeared back inside.

"So, you still have to pull out the costume these days?"

I shook my head as I took another draw from my water glass.

"Not so much. Countermeasures has developed enough of a reputation these days that people take us pretty seriously without me packing my imaginary riding crop."

Cam leaned back in his chair, raised his glass to me. "Now that I noticed. And now that we're signed, you've got to tell me: How do you people get those numbers? I mean literally no one else came even close to you guys."

"We focus on finding the people. I mean, we set up all kinds of screening mechanisms for hardware that might be piggy backing on unsuspecting people or cargo, but it's really Paula's software. It's really more about bad guy detection than weapons detection."

Cam waved my spiel away with his water glass. "Everybody says that. That's what everybody's software does. For the top three bids, the specs were pretty much identical. I want to hear about what's not in the specs. How in the hell can you get it down to a two percent error rate when it comes to reading the human mind?"

I knew the next line in my sales pitch, knew that wasn't what he was looking for. Camden Glaswell was smarter than my average mark. I shrugged.

"Everybody has tie-ins to the same basic databases: international criminal facial recognition, micro-expressions, and suspicious behaviors. It's more math than magic. Our math is just better."

A lie. I knew exactly what gave us the edge. And it was a lot more like magic than math. It was me. Ashley stirred at the suspicious look on Cam's face, but this was Kaitlin's territory.

"Look, you are talking to the wrong member of the team if you want the technical explanation. But here's what I see." I leaned forward, set my elbows on the table, laid my fingertips in my other palm. Made sure he had nowhere to focus but on me. "I see obsession. Paula spends day and night combing the micro-expressions and suspicious behaviors databases, refining them against interview and surveillance footage. She makes me sit in front of the cameras and the monitors for days on end showing me all kinds of video clips. She's got all these code names for every facial muscle, for every combination of facial muscles and she makes all these notes. Then I have to mark when the software made an accurate emotional match. After that she rides her team of programmers for months to make all these obscure changes to the software. I can't tell you what those are. I'm really kept in the dark about that side of the business." I settled back into my chair.

"Why?"

Oh, lovely. I kept my eyes forward, my face smooth. My too-clever mark had me cornered. And I needed to be careful not use too many tricks of the trade. He'd been a cop once. He would recognize them.

The restaurant door. An admiring, slightly jealous caress at my back.

Saved by the waiter.

Justin presented our appetizer and Cam's beer, informed us that he would return momentarily with our main course. The young man was so careful to give us each of us equally courteous attention. Even my brilliant smile of gratitude only threw him for a second, but his relief fluttered over me as he reached that restaurant door.

Cam and I each took a piece of flatbread, tore off strips and began using them to scoop up the pecans, dates, and cheese. Rich and sweet, salty, and crunchy all at once. I sighed.

"Good?" Cam asked with a grin.

I nodded. "Starving."

We ate for a moment in silence. Reminding myself this was the appetizer, I reluctantly pushed the plate toward Cam. He took a few more pieces, then a draw of his beer. I watched him return the glass to the table, trace the condensation across the glass.

"Why are you kept in the dark, Kaitlin?"

Damn.

"Just protecting corporate secrets. Gerard and Jessie met in the Army. It's always been..."

I watched his hand move from his glass to where my fingertips traced the tines of my forks. There it was again, that look in his eyes, so gentle, so earnest. There it was again, that swirl of sensation blasting out from his mind, so hot, so cold.

"It's always been what, Kaitlin?"

He wanted secrets. What would I get for this one? *Give me a clue, Camden Glaswell: How much do you know?*

"It hasn't. I was going to say it's always been need-to-know with them. But it hasn't. Jessie used to encourage me to dog Paula's footsteps, to understand everything about that software. Now he won't let me touch it."

I watched, waited. Tried to ignore the squeeze of hurt in my chest even as I replayed this evening's little hand slap at the bar.

Cam squeezed my hand, kept his eyes to my fingers.

"I don't trust secrets, Kaitlin. Will, he has this story about how the Pilgrims convinced themselves to flee England. He said that they believed God sent signs of his displeasure with the status quo. Relentless and, to them, unmistakable signs. He sent a plague, a huge tidal wave, a drought, and even a spectacular comet. They knew God was telling them it was time to purify his worship. God was telling them it was time to go. Will jokes that the Pioneer Port project has had signs, too. In the form of money. Dozens of federal governments, a whole spectrum of corporations, churches, individuals. This elevator has never wanted for investors. But those investors, those nations and churches, they rely on me. One secret could destroy everything."

Ashley began clawing at the door now, but Kaitlin just shook her head.

"Maybe. But ask those corporations, ask those nations this: Could they function, could they prosper without secrets of their own? It's business, Cam. That's how you make money: by having the better secret."

Our dinner arrived. Cam released my hand, sat back to watch me. He wasn't buying it. What I wanted to see was what he would do with that dissatisfaction.

I lifted my fork, cracked the crust of my pot pie. Steam lifted into the air between us. Cam tapped his fork on his plate in an abrupt rhythm, then sat up to eat. The man attacked his food like it was his first meal of the day. Unfortunately for me, pot pie required a bit more patience. And my second wind was winding down. I picked at the pie as best I could, waiting, knowing Cam would come back around. Silence was an invaluable tool. I just hoped I didn't fall asleep before it worked.

Maybe I actually did fall asleep for a second because the next thing I knew Cam's plate lay empty in front of me. He jumped to his feet.

"I'm going to ask Justin about dessert."

I didn't have the chance to protest. Alone, I stabbed at a carrot, gave up, and set down my fork. The weight of my eyelids prompted me to push out of my chair. Wrapping my hands around my elbows, I wandered to the edge of the woods. Straight up, between the leaves of the young trees, I saw the rich blackness of night dotted with muted stars. Somewhere up there was the space station that acted as a counterweight for the elevator ribbon attached to this boat. A spaceship and a seaship connected by a thin string of nanotubes. In my exhaustion I could imagine the space station pulling us up, up out of the water, a city-sized pendulum swinging at the end of a strand of spider silk, floating away into the stars.

"What are you dreaming about?"

His breath brushed my cheek.

"Space. Floating away on a strand of spider silk into someplace magical."

He chuckled. "You are tired, aren't you?"

I glanced over my shoulder and smiled back at him. He set his hands on my shoulders, lowered his voice to a whisper.

"I think I know what Countermeasures' big secret is, Kaitlin Osgood. It's you. Something about you, but I haven't figured it out yet." His hands moved to cover my shoulders as my heart stopped. "Your skin, your hair. It glows in this light." He was so close, his confused emotions flooded through me.

I shivered, my own mind completely out of focus. Ashley sensed a trap, shrieked at me to run. Kaitlin demanded that I stand my ground and let the game play out to its end. I couldn't breathe.

"Cam, I..." I hesitated as I turned to face him. He let his hands drop to my arms. "I just don't think I'm up to this tonight. I'm so tired I'm starting to see things."

"Let me settle things with Justin and I can walk you to your room."

Now that sounded like a really bad idea.

"Thanks, but I want to touch base with Jessie before I turn in. I forgot to ask him about our schedule for tomorrow."

He watched my mouth as I spoke that little white lie, his own lips gently parted. My stomach turned liquid. I felt myself swaying forward.

I took a deliberate step back. Too fast. This was moving way too fast. Too many unanswered suspicions, too dangerous. I bit my lower lip and looked away, trying desperately to get my head back on my shoulders. It didn't want to go.

"Hey," Cam whispered. He brushed a strand of hair from my cheek, traced my cheekbone with his thumb. I risked a look up at him. I knew Ashley was all over my face. I couldn't help it, couldn't hide it. Cam's blue eyes held only a gentle understanding.

"Hey," I managed.

"So, you need to check in with Jessie?"

I nodded.

"Then let me walk you out."

I smiled, and Ashley slowly faded away again. He released me, and we walked side by side through the restaurant where we bade Justin goodnight. Cam held the front door open for me.

I stepped through, then turned. This time, I was the one laying a hand on his arm.

"Thank you, Cam."

"Thank you, Kaitlin. Hope you get some sleep."

As I walked away, I let my laughter trail behind me down the hall.

4

"Oh, god."

Once again, I found myself staring at the elevator buttons.

Push number nine, go back to my room, huddle in my blankets, savor the sensations of attraction, replay the lingering phrases of our verbal chess match.

Push number twelve, haul Jessie out of bed and report my increasingly clearer readings of random people's intentions. Suddenly, my hallucinations seemed trivial. And Jessie hated it when I talked about what I could do. He was more than willing to rely on my "intuition" as he called it, but when I talked about it in more concrete terms he would get irritated and shut me down. I didn't really want to deal with that right now.

Push number six, see if Jessie was still at the bar. And if he wasn't, I could let it go until morning. Maybe by then it would be over, just the result of some really intense exhaustion.

A good compromise. I hit the button and the elevator began to sink down through the layers of the ship. I rubbed my hands over my arms where the touch of Cam's hands had brought my skin to life.

I think I know what Countermeasures' big secret is, Kaitlin Osgood. It's you. Something about you, but I haven't figured it out yet.

God, what in the hell did that mean? He couldn't possibly know what I could do. That information wasn't in anybody's database, not even in anybody's secret file. Few people from my old life suspected. Even fewer people from my current life had hinted at it.

It's called flirting. Has it been so long?

I put my hands to my face, laughed into my palms. My stomach lowered from beneath my lungs, settled back into the depths of my torso and I knew I had arrived at my destination. I dropped my hands from my face and stepped out into the darkened hall. The thick green carpet was almost black in the low lighting; the faux stone work along the walls became mysterious in its own shadows. This deck was primarily suites. I passed an empty lounge, a vacant play area.

When I reached the little sports pub, the table where Paula had worked lay empty, the bar unmanned. Jessie's massive presence was nowhere to be seen. I turned, ready to make my escape, when I spotted a figure at the back of the bar. His dark green t-shirt and black cargos had acted as camouflage; only the faint ship's light from the window gave him away.

Gerard.

I stopped, watched him for a moment. His larger than life persona had faded. He was too far away for me to feel, but he looked so sad, so lonely. For a second, I nearly forgot myself and stepped out of the shadows to go to him.

"Fuck." He pushed his beer glass away and shoved his chair back.

I stayed where I was and watched him leave. I liked Gerard, didn't want to see him hurting, but he would only ever hear, "Are you alright?" as "Please fuck me." So, I sent him my concern and well-wishes silently. I, of all people, knew how powerful thoughts could be. Maybe it would do him some good somehow.

I retraced my steps toward the elevator. As I passed by the lounge, I saw a group of men—crew members—congregated in their crisp white shirts, ties either loosened or pulled open entirely. My white dress in the ghostly track lighting must have caught their attention. One of them looked up from their soundless conversation, stared me straight in the eyes. I nodded, kept walking.

A cold sweat rushed over me.

Black eyes, shoulder-length wavy black hair. Angular facial bones. Full lips.

I rattled Ashley, demanding a name for that face. All I could remember was...enemy. He shouldn't be here. A name, a name! Ten doors further. Into the elevator and straight to Jessie's room. No. They were following me now, all of them, close enough to read. Their desire to seize me tore at me from behind, claws ripping at my hair, my skirt. My head, the pressure was back—so intense.

A name. He knew me. Ashley knew him.

If I could just try a door, get into a room. Were they all locked? If I stopped long enough to try one, they'd be on me. Ahead I heard a bright, feminine laugh. I looked, a crack of light.

Apologize later.

I shoved my way into the room. I reached back to slam the door.

My head shattered.

Shards of pain exploded like so much glass, leaving behind a tender, exposed emptiness. My shrill gasp echoed through it.

Silence.

The footsteps from the hall followed me in. Someone grabbed my arm from behind as I stumbled forward into the over-bright room. A voice in front of me raised in disgust.

"Mak, what the fuck?! Who the hell is this chick? Are you trying to blow everything?"

I raised my head. The man perched on the arm of the sitting room couch continued to rage at the man gripping me, not giving me a second look. But I saw him, saw the changes wrought both by time and man. Hair once a tousled fuchsia, now hung straight, black to his jaw. A once slender frame now filled in with muscle under that crisp white shirt. The face fuller, more sensual; the eyes still cocky as hell.

Then I felt it, the warmth of his mind touching mine. Him, sliding in, taking over my very being without meeting defense, without facing a moment's resistance.

And he must have felt it, too, because at that instant, Stephan Chen turned to look at me for the first time in five years.

"Ashley?"

5

Kaitlin flickered out and for a moment I did, too. I felt Mak haul my body back onto its feet, saw Stephan slide off the couch and step forward. I regained my balance, clawed Mak's hand away. He just laughed and let me go. He knew as well as I did I wasn't going anywhere.

Stephan and I stood facing each other, too shocked for a real reaction. His gaze searched my face, my body for anything that might confirm what he'd felt. His mind caressed mine, trying to coax out something familiar, some kind of recognition. I clung to my blankness like a knife in a fight for my life.

Slowly, a cold ache poured off him like a despairing mist seeping into my bones. Between us that fog coalesced. The airy specter reached for me, wanting, wanting so much. He would hold me, protect me, nothing would ever hurt me again, he promised me. His wordless whispers filling my head.

Those ghostly arms tried to pull me in.

I jerked back into Mak.

Stephan smiled in triumph.

"Hello, Ash."

So stupid! The blankness in me snapped. I snarled at Ashley, chased her away, even as she stood there looking at Stephan like he was some sort of god. I forced Kaitlin back into consciousness.

"Stephan."

"I like the changes."

He reached out, lifted a lock of my golden hair, let it run through his long, deft fingers. I caught myself watching and jerked my head away.

"I really don't care."

"Ah, but I think you do."

The hands that weren't his hands continued their explorations, tracing my cheekbones, drawing their spectral fingertips down my throat, running their mist-like thumbs along my collarbone. I refused to react. With all my force of will I leveled him a cold stare.

"Let me go, Stephan."

Those cocky eyes just laughed as he smiled.

He looked around the room, sharing the joke, and I took count of the small crowd watching our exchange. Mak with his hands on my shoulders. The three men with him. Two were his, one was ours. A woman, who had hovered in the doorway of the sleeping room, walked in now. Pixie hair, pixie eyes, pixie ears, a tiny, lithe pixie body. Amilee Carson had been frozen in time, down to her elbow-length fingerless fishnet gloves. I saw her eyes tear even as she moved to Stephan's side, put a proprietary arm around his waist.

"You left us," she said.

The girl who had stood by me in the worst times of my life wanted to run to me, wanted to share that old joy with me again. But that joy was too marred with the uncertainty of abandonment, with the fear of losing Stephan. So, she shed silent tears instead.

In that instant, I wanted to grab her, steal her away from here.

Stephan put his arm around her.

I let it go. Let it go like I'd had to five years ago...because I knew she didn't want to be rescued. She didn't see anything to be rescued from. She never would.

Let it go.

"I'm sorry, Ami."

Mak laughed and his sharp fingers dug into my shoulders, a pain that drove much deeper in my flesh, because I knew he wanted so badly to rip me apart. My breath caught in my throat. He dug down to bone, then shoved me aside.

He strode past me to stand next to Stephan, to make sure I understood: the two who had been arch-rivals worked together now, the meticulous safecracker allied with the sociopathic gangbanger. My bile rose.

"With him?"

Stephan smiled grimly. "We've come to an arrangement. This gig was too good to pass up. Mak and his boys have agreed to work for me."

Volcanic rage spewed through the room, knocking my head back. In the fire of his anger, I saw Mak whip out a wicked blade. He grabbed Stephan's arm, rammed the knife into his gut and yanked. Stephan sank to the floor screaming, his hands scrambling to hold the red, fluid life inside him. I saw Mak turn on me, tackle me; one hand tore at my dress as the other hand dragged the knife across my neck.

I screamed.

"Blood! Everywhere. He will betray you. Slaughter."

"What the hell is that crazy bitch doing?"

Stephan grabbed me, shook me. "Snap out of it, Ash. Ashley!"

"I'll snap her out of it. Goddamn fucking zombie eyes!"

I heard the slap of flesh on flesh.

"Don't you touch her."

The fire still beat at my brain, but the vision began to clear. I found myself on the floor, staring into Amilee's eyes. I saw all that old fear, all that old submissive soullessness. A trembling started deep in my chest. Terror. I tore my gaze away.

I pulled myself off the floor. To my left I saw Stephan and Mak exchange blows; in front of me I saw the door covered by a single distracted kid of a guard: one of Mak's. I snapped Kaitlin in place. I charged forward, drove my heel into the kid's foot, rammed an uppercut into his floating ribs. He barely resisted as I shoved him to the floor.

I jerked the door open and ran. I could see the bank of elevators ahead. Which one had I used? The center. I looked at the floor indicator. It was gone. The right-hand one was just two floors away. I slapped the call button, spun around. The other two guards were out the door with Amilee trailing. The cabin door slammed against the wall. Stephan tore out of the room, pushed past Amilee and the two guards.

I fell back against the elevator door. I had nothing to defend myself with, no spritzer, no bag. Shoes. I pulled off my heels, one in each hand. I heard the elevator car settle in behind me. Stephan lunged for me. I shrank back from his grasp, remembered the shoe in my own hand and swung for his head. *He was not getting me back.* Stephan ducked the swing. The elevator dinged. I swung with my left, he caught it, dragged me to him.

"Ashley, stop!"

The elevator door began sliding open. I looked over his shoulder. The onlookers had disappeared from the hall. That warm presence slid along the inside of my skull, fumbling, trying to take over. I yanked wildly at my arm.

"Ashley, it's okay."

"No, it's not!"

I glanced behind me, glimpsed what looked like ship's officers' uniforms in the car. I froze. No one could know. No one ever. Stephan froze, too. I finally managed to pull my hand free, but he ripped the shoe from my grip.

He stood there, holding the glittering white heel like some kind of grisly war trophy as the doors closed over him.

6

"Open the goddamn door, Jessie!" I begged as I watched the peephole for any signs of movement. I couldn't see the elevators from here. Couldn't see if they had followed me, didn't know where the stairs were.

"Come on!" I pounded on the door again.

Finally, I heard the door bolt slide. I released my death grip on the handle as he popped the deadbolt. Jessie opened the door just wide enough to look out. He wore only a hastily thrown on pair of jeans. The rest of him was naked: naked feet, naked torso, naked annoyance. His intention flickered to life inches from my face. I jumped.

Jessie raised an eyebrow. His intention winked out.

"What is it, Kaitlin?"

I tried to answer, but my breath stuck in my chest. I couldn't voice it, couldn't make it real. I jabbed my finger in the direction of the elevators. My entire body began to shake. I had to...I had to...

Jessie grabbed my arm. "Jesus, Kaitlin, what's wrong? What the hell happened?"

He drew me inside, closed the door behind us.

"I...I have to go. I have to go now. He's here. He's found me. I have to go. How do I get out of here? You have to help me get out of here."

"Stephan Chen. Stephan Chen is here on this boat?" Jessie frowned at me. "Kaitlin—"

I held out my arm. Jessie stopped, looked at the scratches and welts left from that final struggle at the elevator. He looked back at my face, then down to my shoulder. The warm push emanating off him turned to a cool, queasy pull. With careful, gentle movements for hands so big, he lifted the side of my hair, slid the shoulder of my dress to the side.

"Oh, baby. What did he—"

Tears welled up. God, not tears. I shook my head, trying shake them away, felt the twist of the bruises for the first time. "Doesn't matter. I've got to go. Please, you have to help me. You don't know what he can do to me. I have to get out of here!"

"Hey, whoa. Whoa there."

Jessie folded me into his arms. My cheek pressed against the warmth of his bare chest. Some distant part of me found it odd. The rest of me just wanted to be safe. I struggled against the air screaming in and out of my lungs, threatening to build into sobs.

"What happened?"

"I went back to...but you weren't there."

"Where? The pub?" His big voice rumbled in my ear.

I nodded.

"He jumped you there?"

I shook my head, my tears smeared across his chest, across my cheek. His arms pulled me in tighter. His pain and panic drove into me.

"Please talk to me, Kaitlin."

I didn't want to hurt him, didn't want to make him worry. I tried.

"One of the rooms. He wanted…"

"What? What does he want, Kaitlin?"

"He's hooked up…hooked up with a rival gang. He said, he didn't say what…"

"He must think you can help him somehow."

I felt the floor drop away. My head fell back from his chest.

"God, Kaitlin!"

"Me. The score means nothing to him. He wants me. Me."

◆

"Shit. Hey, come on back, kid."

I blinked my way back to the surface, the roar of the ocean in my ears. The wild trembling had dropped to erratic shivers. I was lying on the couch. Jessie crouched next to me.

"What the hell was that?"

Ha, he didn't want to hear about the way I could feel people's intentions? Then he *really* didn't want to know what the hell that was.

I put a hand to my head and groaned. It never used to hit me so fast. Jessie would lock me up in the loony bin himself if I kept pulling my oracle routine every time emotions got high.

"Kaitlin?"

I glanced over to the worry in those hazel eyes. I trusted him more than anything in the world. Why didn't he trust me? Maybe because he already knew too much about me. With a sigh, I pushed myself upright on the couch, forcing him to stand up.

"Don't worry about it. Once I get the hell away from him, it won't happen anymore."

Jessie's intentions were strong enough to become corporeal once more. Even as he crossed his arms over his chest, his intention reached down to stroke my hair. I glanced at the door. Stephan had to be somewhere close by.

"I'll be right back," Jessie said.

The layout of Jessie's room was identical to Stephan's. He walked around the end of the couch and into the adjoining sleeping area. A second later he returned, pulling a gray Army t-shirt over his head. He opened a tiny octagonal pot of cream and scooped some out with his finger. He started to reach toward my bruised shoulder, then stopped, scraped the ointment back into the pot and turned it over to me.

"Here. It will help keep the bruising from getting too ugly."

I rubbed a little into each of my tender shoulders. The manufacturer had tried to mask the medicinal scent with lavender. I smoothed a little over the finger marks on my arm just in case. I handed the pot back to Jessie.

He took the pot, stared at it as he rolled it back and forth between his fingers. He lowered himself to the coffee table in front of me. My stomach sank.

"Kaitlin, you told me what you did before you ran. But you never really told me what he did to you back then. And I never asked. It wasn't my place. Plus, it didn't seem like you were really ready to talk about it. But, kid, it's been five years now."

Oh, the shaking was starting again.

I watched my hand run back and forth over the cold bronze upholstery of the couch.

"Kaitlin, did he—"

I shook my head, cutting him off. I tried to look up from my hand on the couch, could only hold his gaze for a second before I looked away again. I didn't want to be this. I didn't want to be like this again. I didn't want to be Ashley with Kaitlin dead, utterly dead inside me. I couldn't even hear her whisper.

"I loved him, Jessie. But he could make me do things I didn't want to do. He..." I shot to my feet. "I have to go." I had to get out of here. I had to get away from here. Go somewhere I could put myself back together again.

I was halfway to the door when I froze. He was out there, somewhere close by.

Jessie's big, gentle hand closed over my shoulder.

"Kaitlin, look at me."

Jessie would never know how much it cost me to turn around, to turn my eyes up to his in that moment. Every cell in my body fought it, but I stood there, I looked him straight in the eye, because I had to. I had to have someone in my life that I could trust that much.

"Do you really want to give all this up? Do you want to give up your career, your apartment, your friends? Do you want to give up the woman you've built yourself up to be? Do you want to give up Kaitlin Osgood?"

Tears again. Goddamn tears again.

"Because if you run again, he's got you. You lose everything, and he's got control of you again. He's followed you all the way out to a boat in the middle of the Pacific Ocean. What does that tell you, Ms. Osgood?"

"That he'll...he'll just keep coming. Oh, god." My knees almost came out from under me right there, but I held on, fought it so hard. I didn't want to be Ashley. Please, don't let me be Ashley.

I stared blankly at the white star in the Army logo on Jessie's t-shirt. He ducked to catch my gaze.

"Maybe it's time to turn around and fight back."

No, no, no. Fighting back would mean being near him. No, no, no.

"My mom—"

"We've got your mom covered." He sighed, pressed his lips together. "Sometimes I think I did the wrong thing, helping you hide."

All the blood drained from my face.

"I don't mean I regret helping you. I mean I regret not trying to convince you to eliminate him as a threat. You can't live like this forever. You weren't strong enough before, but I think you are strong enough now."

Jessie drew me away from the door so very carefully, as if he were drawing me away from a window ledge. "I know it's hard but think about it: he's got just as much to lose as you do with exposure. Let's take our time with this. Let me make some calls tomorrow, see if there is anything we can use. It might even be as simple as showing Cam that he has a record."

"Mak does."

Jessie smiled.

My heart rate slowed for the first time in hours.

"But I don't know his real name. I would have to find an image of him, a fingerprint, something."

I wasn't stupid. It wouldn't be that easy, but maybe, just maybe there was a way...

Jessie chuckled as the calculations played across my face. "Alright project manager. Enough for tonight. It's got to be pushing three o'clock in the morning. Sleep on it. We'll work on it tomorrow."

"Okay. Alright."

Kaitlin hovered at the edge of my senses. As I turned toward the door, I could feel her pushing me to act like a big girl and go.

"I'll walk you," Jessie said behind me.

I sighed my relief, laughed under my breath.

"Thank you."

Jessie disappeared back into his sleeping room, returned with his shoes, sat down on the coffee table. I looked around, grabbed my one remaining heel from next to the door. Jessie raised his head from pulling on his tennis shoes.

"Where's your other one?"

I stared down at the strappy white shoe, over at the scrapes on my arm.

"He's got it."

Jessie's eyebrows rose in alarm as he got up and joined me at the door.

I shot him a wry little smile. "I was trying to use it to put a hole in his temple. You can hardly blame the guy."

Jessie laughed out loud, clapped me on the back.

"That's my girl. Come on, let's go."

◆

"Jessie, I'd know if anybody was here."

"Yeah, but I wouldn't."

My one-room suite wasn't much to search. He flipped back the heavy copper balcony curtains, checked the closet, the bathroom. Unless Stephan was hiding in the box spring, he wasn't here.

"Alright, looks like you're good."

"Yeah, I know."

He reached into the pocket of his jeans, pulled out the tiny pot of cream.

"Keep this. You'll probably need it again tomorrow."

I took it. Then his hand went back into his pocket and came out as a fist. He flipped it over, uncurled his fingers. Nestled in the folds of his palm was a tiny white tablet. One of my sleeping pills.

"Do you want it?"

I hesitated. I really didn't like those things. But I also knew I wouldn't be sleeping at all tonight without it. My fingers looked so small as I picked the pill out of his palm.

"Thanks."

Jessie walked over to the wall pad, tapped on it a couple times.

"I've reset your security to exclude housekeeping and maintenance. Emergency services only." He reached for the handle. "Don't forget to engage the sliding bolt while you're in here."

"Yes, Daddy."

"Alright, then." He looked around the room one more time. "Alright, then," he repeated. His eyes dipped down to the marks on my shoulders. "If you see anything, if anything happens—"

"I'll call. I always do. Goodnight, Jessie."

He nodded. "The bolt," he repeated as he slipped out the door.

I pushed the door the rest of the way closed, flipped the sliding bolt over the hook, twisted the deadbolt into place. As I rested my forehead against the emergency escape sign, a blast of fear and worry slammed into me from the other side of the door. Fear, worry, and just a hint of lust that was quickly quashed. Even in his private mind, my boss believed in propriety. Or maybe part of him really did believe in my little parlor trick.

I turned and looked around the precision tidiness of my cabin, marred only by my bag splayed across the bed.

Not running.

I crossed to the closet, saw all of Kaitlin's clothes hung neatly. Pretty, sophisticated clothes that at first Jessie, then I, had chosen with care to create a confident career woman. Sometimes the only way I could coax Kaitlin back was to go through the purely mechanical motions of being her. So, I eschewed the cotton camisole and shorts and instead pulled out a silk and lace nightgown.

Not running.

My eyes dropped to the suitcase. My breath shook out.

Not running.

I took the nightgown to the bathroom, carefully, precisely brushed my teeth, washed my face, combed out my hair. The comb clattered to the counter as I fumbled it. I straightened it next to my bottle of facial cream, next to Jessie's pot of bruise ointment, next to the pill. I unzipped my summer dress and pulled it over my head. I stared at myself in the mirror. My shoulders and arms were covered with red and purple marks. My eyelids, the hollows of my cheeks were highlighted in greenish black. My eyes were red and swollen.

Oh, god.

No.

Not running.

My arm lit up with pain as I twisted it behind me to unclasp my bra. All of this would hurt so much worse tomorrow. I discarded the bra and slid the nightgown down over me, grateful for the gentle caress of the silk.

It took me three tries to get hold of the pill. I dry swallowed it.

I wandered back out to the room, stared at the bed. I drifted past the door, ran my hand over the sliding bolt, the dead bolt. I lifted the edge of the comforter, let it fall from my fingers. Too vulnerable. So vulnerable without Jessie here to fill up the room. I circled the bed, crossed the sitting area to the balcony window. I flung open the curtains.

No, no bogeyman there. I knew that. I was a hard person to sneak up on.

But she'd done it.

I backed away from the window. My arm wrapped around my stomach; my hand wrapped around my mouth.

I never even knew her name. Just those eyes. The look in those eyes.

I'd told him I wouldn't touch a gun. I told him I didn't even want to be on a run where there was a gun involved at all. But that was Stephan. Never contradicting you. Never forcing you. Just subtly maneuvering everything around you until he had you where he wanted you.

And there I was with a gun in my hand.

Watch the stairs, he said.

Here take this, he said.

It's not loaded, he said.

And there I was at the bottom of the oak stairs in the dark while he and Amilee popped the bedroom safe. I stood in that dark and shook, trying to breathe, hating where I was, who I'd become, unable to fathom how I'd gotten there. Part of my brain said, *Just leave. Just walk away.* But my friends, my best friend and my lover were up there unprotected. They loved me; I loved them. That made them good people, right? Then what were they, what were *we* doing in here violating someone's home, destroying someone's sense of security?

Again.

I stared at the complex metal and plastic firearm in my hand. It felt cold and heavy, toxic in my hand. I didn't want to touch it. Nausea rose in my throat. I started looking for someplace to put the gun down.

That must have been when she walked in.

I heard the foot fall. Such a tiny, quiet sound. But it spun me around.

Such a giant explosion, the gunfire in that tiny space, in that vast silence. Wood splinters sprayed out from the dining room doorsill. A smell like fireworks.

She screamed.

Those eyes stared at me as she screamed and screamed and screamed. Blood gushed down the side of her face, between her fingers as she grasped the side of her head.

I couldn't move.

Stephan and Amilee called my name. The girl crumpled to the floor. The stairs rumbled behind me. Stephan pulled the gun from my hand. I tried—then—to go to her, the staring girl who screamed at the blood running red down her white arms. Stephan blocked my way.

It's one of Mak's girls, he said. *We've got to get out of here.*

He grabbed me. I shoved at him, trying to get past him, trying to get to her.

My screams mingled with hers. *We can't leave her. I shot her. We can't just leave her. She's going to die!*

Stephan silenced my screams with a hand across my mouth. His mind invaded mine, held me limp as he dragged me from the house.

But those eyes came with me.

Those screams, they never left.

7

"Please, please, we have to go back. We can't just leave her!"

"Shh. You're fine. She's fine. Just scratched up a little."

A comforting weight settled into my hair, stroked my head, my cheek.

"We have to..."

"Shh. It's over, Ash. You're safe."

That warm weight settled into my mind. It wrapped around me and held me. The frantic thrashing eased. Peace, an unfamiliar, beautiful tranquility, flowed from the roots of my hair, over my eyes, my cheeks, down through my chest, my belly, out through my limbs.

I shivered, reached one last time for the girl as she faded. A hand grasped mine, lips pressed against my fingers.

"It's okay. I've got you now. You're safe, Ash. You're safe."

◆

I woke only because the sun shone bright enough to pierce my skull even through my eyelids. I groaned pitifully. As I rolled my head to the side, I remembered all too clearly why I hated those sleeping pills. The toxic sludge inside my skull rolled with the movement; the cottony paste inside my mouth had my tongue swollen to twice its normal size. I raised my hand to my face, but the fingers were bloated and barely responsive so much blood had pooled into them during my state of hyper-relaxation.

Sleeping on the couch didn't help.

Today was going to be long and miserable.

Finally giving up, I stretched myself out as much as I could on the slippery little love seat, forcing my muscles to reengage. I caught the comforter before it fell and looked over to the coffee table with its sharp edge dangerously close to eye level. The glass surface was covered with red crumbs. I sat up.

In thick scrawl across the table top was the message:

It's just a door, Ashley.

Next to the message, my tube of red lipstick lay carefully recapped.

"Oh, god."

I looked down at the comforter on my legs. Knew I hadn't put that there. I threw it off of me, scrambled away from the couch. I ran to the balcony window. Jerked at the handle: locked. I sprinted over to the cabin door, checked the sliding bolt and the dead bolt with my eyes and hands.

"How the hell? Oh god, I've got to get out of here!"

I flew back over to the closet, threw open the door. I wrenched my clothes from the rod, hangers and all. Propping up the lid to my suitcase with my elbow, I shoved them inside. I had to drop to my knees in front of the suitcase rack to push and pull at the tangled silk and linen that refused to release the zipper. My shaking hands wouldn't hold still enough to work the threads free from the teeth.

I stopped.

I pulled my hand away and watched it tremble.

You can't live like this.

I gripped the black leather handle of my suitcase and pressed it into my forehead.

"Jessie," I pleaded.

In my mind, he watched me. His arms were folded over that powerful chest, his eyes waited.

I couldn't do this. I couldn't do this to him. I couldn't do this to Paula and Gerard. And Jessie was right; I didn't want to give them up. I didn't want to give up the chance to get to know Cam, to prove that I could pull off this project.

"If I run, I give him the power, but if I stay..."

Don't think about that, Kaitlin warned.

Her voice was strong in my mind. I gripped that strength, pressed my forehead one last time to the handle of the bag, then I drew my feet under me and rose. I looked in the glass mirror of the door. I ignored the wild hair and the beads of saltwater panic shining from my face. In that mirror, I saw what I needed to see: the eyes of Kaitlin Osgood, Senior VP of Sales and Project Management for Countermeasures International. She was smart, she was competent, and she would find a way through this. With the help of her friends. Her real friends.

I strode to the bathroom, pulled out a package of make-up removal pads. Attacking the tissue dispenser, I amassed a giant handful of tissue. I took my arsenal straight to the coffee table.

"Get. Out. Of. My. Room!"

By the time I finished scrubbing that glass not a streak of crimson-tinted castor oil showed, and the entire wad of tissue was stained blood red. I crammed that and Stephan's goddamn message into the garbage can.

When I came back out again, I pulled my bag off the floor and rifled through its leather compartments. I found my mini between a mangled energy bar and a wallet of electronic keys.

Are you still with me? the message flashed. It was ten-thirty already. I had missed the ten o'clock meeting. I was surprised he wasn't beating down the door.

Overslept. Need twenty minutes. Where should I meet you guys?

Setting up temporary office in 5-B. Bring food, he replied.

That was standard operating procedure. We always ate in the office—lunch breaks were for training, but my finger hesitated over the screen. The idea of wandering the ship alone sent snakes slithering through the nerves of my shoulders. Should I tell him about the visitor, about Stephan's little message? I'd promised I would, but if I said anything, I'd probably find myself with a roommate—my boss. That would put Jessie in the middle of it. Just the thought made me nauseous.

But I'd promised.

Kaitlin gritted her teeth and put the mini back in her bag.

◆

Having the billowing gold shower curtain block my view of the room nearly undid my hard-won nerve. The second the last of the conditioner was gone from my hair, I wrenched the water off and flung back the curtain.

No one.

But someone was beating the crap out of my cabin door.

I let out the breath I'd been holding, reached out, and pulled the thick white towel from the rod. I should have known better than to think that Jessie wouldn't worry. Hurriedly, I dried my hair, then wrapped the towel around me as I ran to answer the door. I peered through the peephole, but all I could see was a well-developed shoulder clad in army green. It didn't feel like Stephan or Mak. It felt impatient and a little bit bored. I undid the latches and pulled open the door.

"Gerard?"

My co-boss grinned. "Very nice, Kaitlin. I'll have to volunteer for these errands a little more often." He gave my towel a little tug. I grabbed the top to keep it from falling.

Without giving Ashley a chance to panic, Kaitlin waved him into the room.

"I'll just be about five more minutes."

Gerard strolled in and I closed and bolted the door behind him.

"Oh, don't mind me. I'm just here to enjoy the show."

I began to wonder if Jessie had sent him to annoy the nerves out of me. At least I could be grateful for one thing: no ghostly

imaginings dangled off the front of him. I really didn't need to
see what he wanted to be doing with his hands right now. Could
a person really think about sex that much? Maybe it was a
medical condition. A severe medical condition.

Leaving him to ogle, I tried to pull an outfit from the twisted
heap in my suitcase—one handed. Today would be a manual
labor day. I would need a top that could double—

"Jesus, Kat. What the hell happened in here?"

The sex vibe vanished. Gerard looked from the bed to the
sofa, came over to take a closer look at my suitcase. He lifted a
wooden hotel hanger still entangled in the straps of a blue
camisole.

"Goin' somewhere?" He held the hanger up to me, but
before his gaze reached mine, it hit my shoulder. I hitched my
towel up higher while he stared. My wet hair didn't cover what
by now were some very pretty bruises.

"Those are fingerprints." He dropped the hanger. Anger
burned from his eyes, his body. He pulled out his mini, while
he tossed the room. Like Jessie had, he banged around the closet
door, flipped back the open curtains. Then he headed for the
bathroom, walked out with the wastepaper basket full of red
tissue. Dropping that, he made straight for the coffee table,
grabbed the lipstick tube, opened it and twisted up the mangled
tip for inspection. He even managed to find a streak of message
on the glass that I'd missed.

"Call Jessie," he ordered into the mini.

That spurred me into action.

"No, please." I ran to the sitting area. I pulled at his arm as if I thought I could move it. "Please, Gerard. Don't."

Gerard hesitated, then cancelled the operation, lowered his phone.

"Why?"

"He'll worry. He knows about the bruises already. If he finds out about the rest of this," I waved at the room, "it'll just freak him out. He told me what to do. I'll take care of it. Please." I waited, holding my breath, knowing it was like asking a wife not to tell her husband something. Futile.

He turned to face me, looked down at me for a very long time.

"It's that thing you do with your eyes." I searched his face as he spoke, not understanding. "That's when I can understand why Jessie took you in, why he turned his goddamned world upside down for you." He reached out and brushed his finger tips under my eyes. "It's like there are two women living inside you. One could blast my balls off with a look and the other might disintegrate if I freakin' breathe too hard."

I pulled my hand away and stared at him, feeling utterly exposed in front of the man I had always tried so hard to avoid being vulnerable around. My heart knocked against my breastbone as I took a step back. I gripped the towel tighter to my chest.

"See. That." He waved his hand at me. "I hate that. Fucking pick one. Me, I prefer the boardroom bitch. She's more fun, less work."

I barked out a laugh. "I'll keep that in mind." Would have been funnier, if he hadn't been serious.

I turned away, headed back for the closet. The second I did, the sex vibe was back. I rolled my eyes. The man truly never stopped. Of course, I'd lost half the towel by now. I needed to get dressed, get downstairs, and get re-engaged with life. The day a conversation with Gerard could throw me for an emotional loop was a pathetic day indeed.

The one-armed wrestling match with my wardrobe commenced once again.

"You could just drop the towel."

"Or you could get your useless ass over here and help. Or, even better, step out into the hall."

Gerard grinned. "And miss the chance to pick through Kaitlin Osgood's lingerie? Not a chance."

I turned to glare at him. If he wanted the boardroom bitch, Kaitlin was more than happy to deliver. "Did it ever occur to you that I might have landed you this contract to make it worth my time when I finally sue your ass?"

He only laughed and reached past me into the suitcase. "Here, this should do the trick." He pulled out a red scoop-necked evening blouse—one that would have shown much more than cleavage as I unpacked boxes of equipment. Maybe Jessie really did send him to annoy the nerves out of me. Because I could feel it starting to work.

Gerard held the shirt up to me. I opened my mouth to order him into the hallway when the sex vibe shifted abruptly back to anger and concern.

"Those are fuckin' fingerprints, Kaitlin! Did you write all over the frickin' coffee table or was it this guy? What did it say?"

It's just a door, Ashley.

And that door began closing over my mind, darkness filling up the outer edges. Ashley welcomed the escape, the release. Even Kaitlin offered little resistance.

"Whoa, okay. Don't do that. God, Jessie would kick my ass from here all the way back to Miami. Shit. Don't you fuckin' do that."

I caught myself on his arm. I shook my head out, embarrassment flooding my cheeks. Had I almost fainted in front of Gerard "Horndog" O'Connell? Could this day get any worse?

I gingerly patted the grab marks out of the sleeve of his T-shirt, staring as though this required all my concentration. "I...I need to not talk about this for a little while. Alright?" Sparks of darkness still flew in my vision.

"Ya know what? I'm gonna go out in the hall."

And rat me out. Great.

8

Jessie didn't say anything through the three hours we spent hauling boxes from the warehouse-sized cargo area and organizing them in our narrow little workspace. Of course, he didn't have to. I thought my back would light on fire he was so pissed. Fortunately for me, I was the one with all the tracking information for our freight, so I spent most of my time in the cargo area locating boxes.

Unfortunately for me, when I got down to the last three boxes, no amount of searching yielded Gerard's precious surveillance cameras. And I'd forgotten my mini with its tracking reader back in the conference room.

The second I closed the conference room door behind me, the second Jessie realized I was alone, I could feel the change in the air. He turned to face me.

"You lied to me."

I offered a small smile. "I never got the chance to actually lie about it."

Jessie raised an eyebrow.

I sighed. "What did Gerard tell you?"

"That when he got there your room was trashed and your clothes were wadded up in the suitcase with the hangers still on them. He said somebody had written something all over your coffee table in lipstick, but when he asked you about it, you about passed out on him."

I opened my mouth. Closed it again.

"Kaitlin, what happened?"

I looked up at him with his thick arms crossed over his chest. His face had set into hard lines. Ashley quietly suggested we slip back out the door.

"Don't you do that. You stand up straight, look me in the eye, and answer me."

It took a serious force of will, but Kaitlin left Ashley to cower alone in the cave in the back of my mind. She snapped into place under my skin. Unfortunately, that had little effect on my mouth.

"Stephan got—" I cleared my throat. "Ah, well, Stephan got into my room last night. I'd already taken my sleeping pill. I only remember fuzzy images." Stephan leaning over me; Stephan stroking my hair, my face, tucking the comforter around me. "But when I woke up, I saw that message on the table. I flipped out."

"Started packing?"

I nodded.

"What did the message say?"

That broke the eye contact. Clutching my workpad tighter, I stared at the box to the right of his head, a big box with identifier: Paula, Box 3. I knew from my freight list that it contained all the parts for her interview scanner. Except the software plug-ins. Those were in Box 1 with the backups in Box 5.

"What did it say, Kaitlin?"

Don't think about it, just say it.

"It's just a door, Ashley."

"It's just a door," he repeated quietly.

That precise control he always kept on his emotions snapped like a lightening bolt tearing through the room. I jerked back.

"That's it. You're bunking with me. If he likes—"

"Don't. Stop. Just stop. This is exactly why I didn't tell you. I don't want him knowing how much you know. I don't want you in the middle. These are my mistakes rearing up to bite me in the ass."

"So, you're just going to put a sign up on your door, 'Come on in'?" The anger on his chiseled face, radiating flare-like off his entire body, made me forget for a moment what I was trying to say.

"No, I...I was going to do what you told me to do."

"Kaitlin, he broke into—"

He wasn't the only one who could get angry. I held up a hand. Now I was standing up straight, looking him straight in the eye. Both Kaitlin and Ashley stood tall in me, though Ashley quivered so hard I didn't know if I'd be able to follow through. If I was alone, Stephan would be back. Could I handle it? Somehow I had to.

"I'm not going to take everything you've given me and use it to destroy your life."

"I didn't give it to you, so you could throw away yours."

"I'm not going to. He wouldn't hurt me—physically. Not on purpose."

"Those bruises were signs of affection?"

The vent above me began roaring dully. I stepped out of the stream of air that patted my hair.

"He didn't do that. And I've gotten worse in training." No mentioning Mak. Not ever mentioning Mak.

"Kaitlin—"

"I'll leave. If I have to, I'll leave." I felt my eyes prick, but I was done with tears. "I won't risk you."

Jessie stepped forward, wrapped his big hands around my upper arms left bare by my sleeveless black button shirt. "Kaitlin, you're shaking."

I took a deep breath, forced the tremors to cease. I raised my gaze back up from his white T-shirt to his eyes.

"You said I was strong enough. So, I'm going to be strong enough."

In the small gap between us, the warmth of pride pushed out from him and into me. A brief spike of lust. Then he lowered his arms and stepped back. For the longest time he looked around the room as if memorizing the positions of the boxes stacked tight around us. Finally, those hazel eyes turned their drill sergeant gaze back down to me.

"Two conditions. One: you strap on an 'oh shit' button at all times. And two: you let Gerard rig a camera in your room."

My stomach did a quick flip and I let Ashley indulge in one final pathetic wish that he had tried harder to talk me out of it. God, how was I going to do this?!

I nodded.

Immediately his finger jabbed down in my face. "You ever hold back from me again, this is over. Money isn't more important than lives, Ms. Osgood."

"Yes, sir."

I was never going to be able to keep both promises to him. He had to know that. But the lecture was over. Behind me the door creaked open. Apparently, you didn't have to be part oracle to feel the tension in the room.

"Ah, Kaitlin," Paula hesitated. I unhooked my clawed fingers from my workpad and tried to erase the chastised teenager look from my face. I turned to see her head sticking through the door, the gleam of her mahogany hair spilling to the side.

"Yeah?"

"Gerard wants—"

"The tracker. I'll be right there."

"Great. Thanks."

Paula popped back out again. I looked around, spotted where my bag had been stuffed under a chair on top of the conference table. I reached down the side and found my mini completely wrapped in the gleaming silver of my energy bar. I sighed and pulled them apart. That thing had to be expired. I was never going to eat it. I eyed the recycling can next to the door. But back in it went.

As I reached for the door, Jessie called over his shoulder from where he tapped away at his workpad, "This room is too small. Talk to Mr. Brands. And tell Gerard and Paula we're meeting for training in twenty."

"Yes, sir."

And then I fled.

◆

"What the hell am I supposed to do without the damn cameras?"

"Gerard, they're not here. Maybe they just missed the boat. Give me a second and I'll see if I can find where they ended up." I stuffed the mini in the pocket of my capris and took my workpad back from Paula. I leaned back against the cargo rack, grateful for the thin fabric of my shirt and the metal which was at least five degrees cooler than the air around it.

Paula pulled her own mini out. "It's time. We need to go hook up with Jessie."

Training time was sacred at Countermeasures. Everybody from the techs to the receptionist was expected to participate. VPs and presidents were not exempt from this company ritual either.

I followed Gerard out of the steady, draining heat of the hold and into the hallway. Paula shivered. I smiled sympathetically. The over-air-conditioned public areas on the operations side of the ship made for a miserable temperature transition.

"I keep wondering if they do it to keep the popsicle people from thawing out when they have to move them from the lab," Paula muttered, wrapping her arms around herself as we waited for the elevator.

Gerard and I laughed. The nice thing about Gerard, his tantrums never lasted long. He didn't have the attention span for it. The elevator arrived, and we settled in. At least the operations-side elevators weren't full of mirrors.

"Dude," Gerard clapped his hands together. "When is the tour calendar-girl? I wanna see the inside of that cryogenics lab. And the elevator, do you think they'll let us take a ride up to the space station? I want to see the docks where they're building the voyagers. Maybe they'll have one ready. Maybe we could see inside one."

"I'm supposed to schedule the tour with J.C. as soon as we get our office put together. But there won't be any elevator rides any time soon. They're still in the last stages of building up the ribbon."

"But we're here for six months!" Gerard's burst of disappointment even made me feel sad. And I had no intention of ever setting foot in that thing. He joked often enough about how much he missed playing human dirt dart out of the military airplanes. Maybe he actually meant it. The elevator settled on the fifth floor and he held the door for Paula and me as we stepped out.

"They'll be running manned elevators before we leave, but it takes a whole week to get up there," I said.

Both Paula and Gerard turned to me as we rounded the last corner before the conference room.

"Wow," Paula mouthed.

"Neither of you read the report I put together on this project?"

"I did," Paula objected.

"I didn't. Didn't have any blueprints in it. What the hell good was it gonna do me?" Gerard dropped back, and I found myself with a muscular arm draped over my neck. "But hey, I heard you sweet talking ol' J.C. into letting us open up the airwall in the conference room. You two are pretty tight, right? You could loosen him up for me. Maybe offer a couple of sexual favors in exchange for a ride on the ol' sling shot to the sky."

I lifted Gerard's arm from my shoulders and dropped it.

"This," I replied as I opened the door to the conference room, "would be why I do the sweet talking and you do not."

Behind us, Paula walked into the room with a little chuckle that turned into hysterical laughter. Jessie looked up from packing his workpad into his bag.

"What?"

Paula and I exchanged an evil smile and she waved Jessie's question away.

"Ready to go?"

The three of us dug our respective bags out of the crannies where they'd been stuffed to make room for the overload of boxes which had begun to make the air reek decisively of high school locker room: musty and damp, turning to mildew.

Jessie set the door to lock as we headed out. As he locked step with me, I felt Kaitlin falter. Carefully, trying not to let him sense it, I settled her back into place. Kaitlin didn't carry a reprimand with her like baggage. She changed course and moved on. It would have been a lot easier if the man next to me had done so as well. But then he hadn't been in the hold arguing with Paula and Gerard. He'd been alone in the conference room stewing.

"I talked to J.C. He said we could go ahead and open up the airwall and take over the room next door if we need to."

Jessie nodded.

Well, that went well.

We all climbed onto the elevator. And stood in silence for the duration of fourteen floors.

When we finally arrived at the employee gym, we discovered there were no locker rooms associated with the facility. Jessie sent Paula and me in to change first while he and Gerard waited outside. We switched with the boys and dumped our bags against the wall.

Paula peeked over at me.

"Just how much trouble are you in for missing the meeting this morning? It was just a stupid meet and greet."

I flashed a pained smile. If that's what she thought was going on, so much the better.

"I was supposed to run that meeting with Cam."

"He was asking about you."

My body flashed back to the sensation of his palms resting against my skin, his breath in my hair. A delicate, beautiful moment I'd misplaced in the disaster the rest of the night had become. I savored the memory for just a moment. "I'm sure he was," I murmured.

I caught the hum of fretting buzzing off of Paula and looked over to her.

"Don't worry. He'll get over it," I assured her.

She looked apologetic. "I know."

Despite the fact that she wasn't my report, I still felt the need to shield her when things got too testosterone-laced. I'd hired her, so I felt responsible for her. Which was ridiculous because she was probably older than I was, but she was so delicately feminine—even in yoga pants and a muslin tunic. She was brilliant, but like a lot of brilliant people, she was also brilliantly focused, so in the end our connection was loose. The most I knew about her was that she was a single mother of a seven-year-old boy named Brian who would be joining us here when our install people, India and Andrès, came down after Brian finished his visit with the grandparents.

The door cracked.

"Come on in!" Gerard said, already walking away.

Paula and I crossed the aerobics floor and dropped our bags by a rack of barbells on the far side of the small room. I spotted a treadmill and decided I could work on following the electronic trail of Gerard's precious cameras while I worked up a sweat. After a quick set of stretches, I grabbed my workpad and made a beeline for the machine.

I had just figured out how to bypass all the automatic settings when Jessie walked up beside me. He pushed cancel and I had to move quickly to keep from falling as the belt abruptly slowed.

"Not today. Come on."

Ah, shit.

I tried to reason with him. "Jessie, some of our boxes have gone missing."

Oh, damn, the box with the cameras. Like the camera that he wanted to install in my room, I realized abruptly. Crap.

"Later."

He was already walking toward the aerobics floor. I tapped my thumbs on the sides of my workpad, then gave up and followed him. Ashley began pacing behind her closed door as I dumped my pad into my bag and stepped onto the floor. Gerard jumped and kicked in the upper right-hand corner of the space, watching his form in the mirror. Paula pedaled away at the stationary bike, engrossed in a novel on her workpad.

I squared my shoulders as Jessie turned. He reached down and took my wrist in a loose grip. By rote, I bent my elbow, rotated my wrist up and over his thumb. His hold broke. Other hand, up and over. He got a grip on the thick spandex of my workout tank top. I rammed the heels of my palms up into his elbows, circled outside to the chop down on the crooks of his arms. Then one fist drove forward toward his solar plexus while the other chopped toward his throat. His hands released my clothes.

"Choke holds."

God, I hated this. His arm was thicker than my neck was long.

Jessie stepped behind me. In the mirror I watched him position himself, a full head taller and half body wider than me. Ashley began to make sounds of panic then, but it wasn't until he laid one hand on my shoulder and I felt those bruises stab into me that the fear prickled to life on my skin.

"This... this isn't going to work, Jessie."

"Sure it is. You're doing great."

I looked into his eyes in the mirror as he wrapped his arm snuggly around my windpipe. I mocked cracking backward with my head (as though I could have possibly reached his nose), then scraped my training shoe down his shin, shifted my hips to the right and rolled him off my fulcrum point and onto the floor. His arm conveniently left my neck as he fell.

"Because you don't hate me," I whispered.

I stepped around him, walked over to Gerard, heard Jessie jump to his feet behind me.

"Come after me like you meant it."

"Oh, no, I'm not getting in the middle of this."

"I'm giving you a free pass. Get it all off your chest."

I saw Gerard look to Jessie and receive a subtle nod. He thought he could pounce while I wasn't looking. He forgot that I could see with more than my eyes. I ducked to the left and ran. I shot past Jessie and Gerard lunged for me. Our shoes shrieked across the wood floor as I twisted out of his reach and sprinted to put the workout machines between us. I got to the other side of the stair stepper, spun around to face him. His face, his body was utterly focused. But he didn't hate me.

He feinted to the right. I feinted to mine. He decided to risk coming up and over. The moment he got that second foot off the floor, I crouched down and shoved. The overbalanced machine went toppling over and he went with it.

Now he was pissed.

"Fuckin' shit!"

I heard him scrambling to his feet. I reached the other side of the circuit training machine and he was after me. No feinting now. He charged at me, his anger licking at my back as I jumped the fly bench and headed for the aerobics floor. As I glanced back over my shoulder, I saw him launch off that bench.

He had me.

He caught my arm first and no amount of levering or circling could break his hold. Spitting curses, he twisted my arm up behind me. Kaitlin had had her turn; now Ashley fought dirty. Rearing back, I went for a head butt to the nose. He had to release my twisted arm to get his face out of the way, but his hand caught my arm again higher. He felt my tell as I went for the groin shot. He body slammed me to the floor.

"Jesus Christ, Kaitlin!"

Gerard's 215 pounds had every square inch of my 125 pinned to the ground, completely immobilized. My lungs felt empty and every breath I tried to pull shrieked ineffectually through my throat. Gerard stared me down nose to nose.

"Are we fuckin' done now?"

I nodded. *Yes,* I told Ashley, *we are fucking done now.* Almost as if exhausted, she slipped off into her darkness.

Gerard's muscles bunched over mine, then he was up on his feet. I curled to my side and the wheezing eased. Sitting up, I tucked my feet under me and found a hand dangling of my face. I looked up. Gerard's intentions felt blurry to me—but that was probably more the ringing in my head than him. I put my hand in his. He pulled me to my feet.

I had to dig my toes in and lock my knees to keep from wobbling. Gerard used our joined hands to pull me in. When he had me in one of those one-armed guy embraces, he whispered in my ear.

"You okay?"

"Yeah. You?"

He just made a snort of derision in reply. I turned as he let me go to return to his workout. I stood looking at Jessie who still stood where I'd left him in the middle of the aerobics floor. His emotions hadn't settled yet. I caught anger, frustration, sadness, even a thread of jealousy.

I pulled my gaze away, walked off the wooden floor. I grabbed my workpad where it stuck out from my bag. As I passed Paula, her tendrils of fearful discomfort coalesced into a thick guilt in the pit of my stomach. I gave her arm a squeeze and returned to my treadmill.

I didn't have the muscle to upright the stair stepper, so why even bother trying.

I hit the resume button and turned my attention to the package tracking window on my workpad. Those damn cameras had made it as far as Ecuador. I would post a query, but I'd bet a month's wages that $50,000 worth of cameras had been garnished from our shipment as a customs "gratuity."

I opened my mouth to tell Gerard. Stabbing pains shot through my chest; my throat constricted.

Just had to do it. Just had to pop off and erase any illusion that I could somehow, someway protect myself from Mak and

Stephan. Just had to shatter the delusion that I wasn't utterly vulnerable no matter what I knew or did. Just had to.

I stepped off the belt and froze, lips pressed together.

Carefully, Kaitlin shut down the machine. Trying not to hurry, she walked over to her bag and slung it over her shoulder. Without looking around at the awkward silence I'd created, she crossed the aerobics floor and pushed through the heavy door.

I'd be damned if I was going to let them see me cry.

9

I had the airwall open and the boxes rearranged before they made it back. I considered my duty done. I made my escape.

In the hospitality section of the ship, I followed the signs to a food court. To my surprise, the seating area was not empty, but held about twenty-five other people, maybe more. Some were obviously staff—families with kids, some obviously investors—suits with too perfect grooming, but the rest were contractors like me. I felt very underdressed in my gym clothes.

It didn't help that the pack of teenagers ahead of me in line for the sandwich shop kept stealing glances for the full ten minutes of my wait. Nothing more intimidating than a pack of moody, hormonal teenagers. Especially when you don't have to guess where their thoughts are ricocheting.

But no sign of Stephan or his little band of thieves.

And I felt like a thief by the time I got back to my room, hunkering down over my sandwich behind locked doors. I felt restless and furtive, stupid for running out on everyone. I knew the smartest move was to stay put, work through a concrete plan on how to extricate Stephan and Mak from my life. I knew that. But Ashley prowled in my brain, back and forth, back and forth, making it so hard to concentrate. I perched on the edge of the couch and picked at the lettuce that had fallen from my sandwich onto the smeared and tattered wrapper.

I heard Kaitlin's sole command.

Commit.

I jumped to my feet. Wading up the wrapper, I walked to the bathroom and stuffed it in the garbage can. I pulled a cami and shorts from the pile hanging out of my suitcase. Shower, brush teeth, change into pajamas—all definite markers of staying in. At the threshold of the bathroom I glanced back at my wall pad, pretended I wasn't wishing for a message from Cam, pretended I wasn't wondering why I hadn't heard from him all day. Promised not to call him—not yet, not tonight.

Commit.

◆

Settled back in the abundant pillows of my bed—where I could see both the doors with the slightest turn of my head—I began to research what I had missed in the last five years. In hiding, I had cut every tie to the street punks who had been my world. Now I had to reconstruct the web that had led them back to me.

Stephan Chen.

Through the licenses I'd secured for Pioneer's Port, I had access to databases most security firms could only dream of getting their hands on. The International Criminal Information Center was probably too big time for a local like Stephan, but it had been five years. And here he was poised on the cusp of *something* international in scope—even if it was just international trespassing. Maybe it wasn't the first time he'd tried something like this.

My heart drummed against my sternum, making it hard to breathe as I entered his name into the search form. Gripping the sides of the workpad, I waited for the bits and bytes to cross two oceans and a couple continents to some undisclosed location in Europe.

Results: 4 matches.

"Okay, here it goes."

I clicked on the results and read through the macro-level particulars. I laughed at my reaction. Of course not. Three Stephan Chens born in the 1900s and one very dead nineteen-year-old. I reached up to close the window, then hesitated over a birth date: January 13, 1991.

1991.

I clicked on it.

I skimmed. Taiwanese drug trafficker. Taipei to Seattle. Presumed dead in skirmish with U.S. Coast Guard, February 25, 2031.

His dad. Could that be his dad?

Quickly I copied the data over to a local file.

Bang. Bang. Bang.

My workpad flew off my lap and landed facedown at the foot of my bed. Quickly, I scrambled after it and closed down everything I was working on. I dropped the pad on my nightstand and peered through the peephole. Why did I always feel like I was asking to be shot through the eye every time I did that?

Gerard looked back at me with one eyebrow raised.

Wonderful.

I slipped Kaitlin on like the robe I wished I had and opened the door. Gerard looked me up and down.

"Not bad, but I liked the towel better. Here, catch!" He tossed me a pole—no a curtain rod—forcing me to release the door to catch it. Then he proceeded to barge in, carrying a trendy metal chair, identical to the ones I'd seen in the food court.

"What are you—"

"Figured after you tried to murder me with that girly workout machine, you owed me one. So, I'm here to collect a pole dance. Better make it good." He swung the chair around, dropped his ass into it.

I just stared. His intentions didn't have any of that greasy sickly feeling to them, so I simply stood and waited. And considered taking the pole to the side of his head. Then I felt that first little shift to serious.

I sighed, dropped the pole across the bed.

"I'm sorry."

"Yeah, well, next time you have a point to prove, don't use me to do it. I didn't like that. It was nasty. Gave me the creeps. Especially with all this going on." He gestured to my two apparently useless doors.

Then the seriousness switched back off again and he jumped to his feet. "Damn, the Bride of Frankenstein actually apologized. This is a day for the record books!"

"Bride of Frankenstein?"

Gerard laughed. "That's what I call you when I really want to piss Jessie off. Works every time."

"Bride of Frankenstein."

"Or Build-It-Yourself Barbie."

"Gerard, you are a jackass. Consider the apology retracted."

He just grinned and hauled the curtain rod off the bed. "So, Dr. Frankenstein found out we're out a bajillion dollars worth of video equipment, so he sent me here to secure the room the old fashioned way."

He crossed over to the balcony window. Holding the rod up to the recessed section of the window, he measured, then marked it off. Gerard planted his giant boot in the middle of my coffee table, balanced the rod across his knee, and used a laser saw to destroy Port property. When he was finished, he dropped the shortened rod into the sliding glass door's track.

But the vandalism was not yet complete.

Back on the other side of the room he applied the laser saw to the rounded back of the metal chair, cutting out a divot that precisely matched the neck of the cabin's door handle. Then he sawed off the sliders on the chair's feet, leaving the sharp metal edges exposed.

"You get the idea here?" he asked, gesturing to the remains of the chair.

"Yeah, just shove it up under the door handle."

"There we go."

He collapsed the laser saw and returned it to the holster on his belt.

I looked from the door handle to the dead bolt to the sliding bolt and my stomach begin to quiver. As much as Gerard annoyed me, I almost didn't want him to leave.

"How did he get in, Gerard?"

Gerard folded his arms over his chest and followed my gaze.

"My best guess is through the balcony window. Be easier and faster than dealing with all this hardware."

I pictured Stephan in the dark dangling nine stories over the open ocean. I shook my head. "Insane."

"You're cutting into my beer time, Osgood." He held up remaining stub of the curtain rod. "Unless you've changed your mind about the show?"

"Out."

I held the door open for him. As he passed by, he gave my cami a little tug.

"How 'bout something with a little more lace next time?"

"Goodnight, Gerard."

And I shut the door in his grinning face.

Bang. Bang. Bang.

And I opened it again.

"What?"

Gerard dug into his pocket and pulled out a wrap-around bracelet.

"Forgot this. Your 'Oh, Jessie, please save me. Oh, Jessie, please.'"

I grabbed the "oh shit" button bracelet out of his hand, used it to point down the hall in the direction of the elevators.

"Beer, Gerard. Goodbye, Gerard."

"Don't forget the lace, Osgood."

I slammed the door in his face.

Jackass.

But even Ashley couldn't work up the enthusiasm to hate him.

10

10:02 p.m.

I realized I'd been staring at variations of that number for the past fifteen minutes. With a resigned sigh, I shut down my research. I felt fairly confident that I had tracked down Stephan's family. Dead parents and a sister with a birth certificate and only a couple of years of elementary school to her name—then nothing. That sounded right. Through the haze of distant memory and present exhaustion I thought I remembered a white-hot hatred of his father, a tearing sadness for his mother. The sister was a more guarded memory of his, less specifically mentioned than inferred.

I reached out and laid my workpad on the nightstand. After a few minutes of coaxing, I managed to get myself up off the bed to reassure myself with Gerard's makeshift security system. I laughed at the sawed-off chair and wondered exactly how much trouble that was going to get me into—because I knew Gerard would never take responsibility for it.

Just to prove I was that brave, I turned my back to the door and wandered into the bathroom for some water. I stared at myself in the mirror.

So, I had Stephan digitally ID'ed. So far that hadn't done me any good. It was like I'd told Jessie. Stephan was a very, very careful thief. Coming here after me, that just didn't fit. Unless he had a very legitimate-looking cover. But if getting him on falsifying employment records was going to be my tactic, I was going to have to be patient. I didn't have access to the port's employment records yet. And that could be weeks.

The thought sent a tiny tremor running through my gut. Inside my brain, Ashley resumed her relentless pacing like a caged animal that was quickly losing its mind.

Shit.

I wasn't going to be able to sleep.

I filled my cup with tap water and walked back out to sleeping area.

"Where do you think you are going?"

"Oh, god!"

The water glass shot from my hand and shattered on the chair still wedged securely under the door handle.

In the amber lamp light, Stephan stood gazing speculatively into my suitcase. Slowly, he drew a lavender and purple silk scarf free from the interlocked hangers and suit jackets. Playing the silk between his fingers, he turned to me.

"You know there's not another ship due out for four days. Did you forget to mark your escape routes, Ashley? Have you forgotten everything I taught you?"

He cocked his head to the side, slid me a slow smile. My stomach clenched. Ashley slipped a little from my hold as she sang to that smile. God, he was beautiful. Even more beautiful than that morning when he'd first coaxed me from the train my second year of college.

Stupid, naïve, fool.

"How the hell did you get in here?" I whispered.

"Were you going to run away from me?" He started circling, putting himself between me and the door. "I always thought you ran because of that girl. Did I have it wrong?"

He was getting closer now. I skirted away toward the closet. Jessie's button! I glanced to the night stand.

"You looking for this?" Stephan held up the bracelet, then slipped it back in his pocket. "I think we'll leave them out of this little conversation for now."

He took a step toward me.

I had nowhere to step back to. I lost my breath for a second when my back hit the closet.

"I waited five years for you to come back, Ash." His mind gently brushed mine, a tender touch.

"Don't."

He lost his careful grip on his thoughts, his emotions. No one can hide it from me completely, not for long. Some of it slipped free, some of it coalesced between us as a dream of him, reaching out, cupping my face.

"Stephan."

He was in.

I swayed with it, with the warmth, with the peaceful completeness of it as Stephan refilled that empty part of me, drained away the fear and the anger. Somewhere, somehow, I knew I should fight it. Kaitlin's echoing warning, fading away.

But it felt so good. Ashley unfurled within me, drinking in the safety, the certainty that poured from Stephan into me. She was loved. Completely. She could finally be free.

Then the strength of his real arm came around my waist, the heat of his real fingers tunneled into my hair.

"I took care of you; I protected you; I loved you." His lips traced over my cheek. "This is what we were together, Ashley. Neither of us will ever find this with anyone else. How could you leave? How could you leave me?"

I looked into his eyes, saw the pain, the desperation there. He brushed his lips like a whisper over mine, then sank into me. Ashley rose to meet him, a reunion of souls. And as Ashley drifted in bliss, Kaitlin stepped forward.

Stupid, naïve, fool.

I found just enough control to turn my head away.

"Don't, please."

Stephan stumbled with me past the closet, clutched my head as he forced me to look at him.

"Why did you leave, Ashley? Tell me why you left me."

We landed against the wall, his body pressed into mine. His hands left my face, wrapped around my ribs, just below my breasts. With each stroke up and down my body his thumbs reached higher.

"Why, Ashley?"

"I didn't...want..."

"Want what, Ashley?"

"I didn't want to die."

His hands stilled, cupped along the sides of my breasts. He pulled his face away to look into my eyes.

"I would never, ever hurt you, Ashley. You know that."

His left hand closed over my breast, his right hand pulled me hard into him. Ashley gasped. Kaitlin screamed.

Tears touched my cheeks. Frantically, Kaitlin tore at the fog in my mind. I couldn't let him do this. I couldn't let him do this to me again!

I twisted my head away from him, but he simply lowered teeth, lips, and tongue to the neck I'd exposed. I got my hands between us and shoved. All my effort simply pushed me harder back against the wall.

I could feel him reclaiming that tiny tract of clarity Kaitlin had won as he slid the straps of my cami from my shoulders.

No, please! I'd tried so hard, fought so hard. I couldn't survive this again!

"Let me go." A pathetic whimper. "Please, let me go! LET ME GO! LET ME GO! LET ME GO!"

In a blind frenzy I struck out at him, the frenzy growing wilder as Kaitlin felt his hold falter.

"Ashley, stop. Stop! I'm not going to hurt you, Ashley. Calm down. What's wrong?"

"Don't touch me. Don't touch me." I wrenched away from the wall, but he had my arm and that fucking circle lever move didn't work on thief hands either.

"Get your hands off me!" I screamed and threw my full body weight into yanking against his hold.

He released me.

I fell back, hit the edge of the bed. Immediately, I scrambled backwards. I hit the headboard and pulled my limbs against me. I froze there, shaking so hard the bed rattled in its frame. Stephan stood unmoving at the end of the bed, arms limp at his sides.

Finally, he spoke.

"You left because of me. You are...you are terrified of me."

The soul-deep hurt that came over that usually cocky face unlocked years of rage.

"You destroyed me! You turned me into someone I hated! You fed me drugs and alcohol like they were fucking candy! You dragged me into people's homes while you ripped off the things they'd worked so hard for. You made me help you...help you make them fear being in their own goddamn homes! I couldn't look in the fucking mirror it made me so sick to see what you'd made me into. Sick! So, don't fucking tell me you didn't hurt me. There wasn't any part of me left by the time you fucking got done with me!"

Stephan stared at me in shock.

"Ashley," he whispered.

The words, held so long secret, were gone. With a wordless scream, I collapsed in on myself. I felt the cries and sobs as they ripped through my throat. I felt the incredible pain as it ripped through my body. I gripped my knees to my forehead and rocked, fighting through that pain for the short, sharp breaths I caught. If the pain could just take me apart, take me away. I couldn't take this killing fear anymore.

I felt cold fingers press against my shoulder.

I screamed and jerked away.

"Shh, Ashley. Ashley."

Tentatively, he reached out with his mind. This time it was his intention that brushed against my shoulder.

"No!"

"It's okay, Ashley. I'm just going to..."

Lightning fast, he seized me. My body went rigid; my mind went blank. A shuddering convulsion racked my frame as my body reacted to the rapid transition. Then slowly my body settled, relaxed into the pillows, into his hands as he pulled me to him. He wiped my face with his shirt sleeve and settled my empty form against his chest.

He kept that vise-grip on my mind as he rocked me, murmuring quieting nonsense. From somewhere beyond my battered body, beyond the endless battlefield of my mind, I watch him hold me, felt his lips move against my forehead, heard him chanting.

"Shh, it's okay. I'm so sorry. I didn't know. I never knew that's how you felt. How could I have not known? You hated my Ashley. How could anyone hate my Ashley? Oh, god."

So far away, a curiosity and nothing more. It was so good to float here, just me, no more Kaitlin, no more Ashley. Just me and that sad, confused man down there.

"I have to go. I can't leave you like this. God, please don't hate me. I couldn't let you hurt so bad. I'm going to help you sleep. I'll stay with you just until you sleep."

No need for sleep. Sleep was reality. Reality was bad. Here was just fine. Very, very fine.

But the man could coax blood from stone. So slowly he transformed his hold on my mind from rigid entrapment to a soothing, so soothing embrace. That gentleness was wonderfully alluring, but my *away* was better...far, far away. Patiently, he stroked my hair, stroked my face, rocking me.

At the edge of my awareness I saw an image, heard a sound. His voice, my face—younger, innocently younger. That first fateful train ride. It's misting outside the tinted window. He leans over and asks me if I want to play hooky. I look up from my workpad, just a kid with bright eyes and a pretty smile. And he knows. This is the one.

Later.

The first time at his one-room apartment. Just a little bit nervous, embarrassed about the peeling paint and lack of furniture. He answers the door and there I am standing in front of him with the prettiest spring dress with tiny blue flowers and my wild brown hair is tamed into a low bun at the back of my neck and he thinks I'm the most beautiful thing he's ever seen. And a perfect peace settles over him.

Later.

Meeting my mom. He's thinking the house is so tiny and old, but it has been well cared for. He pulls open the warped screen door with its rough blue paint. Then my mom opens the inside door to welcome him. I step up beside her and give him a reassuring smile. All he can think is that this is how beautiful, how sweet his Ashley will be as we grow old together.

Slowly, the memories become my own. Slowly, I settle the sheets more comfortably around me. Slowly, the memories become dreams.

11

"Wow, somebody needs to get laid."

I snarled at Gerard through the blue plastic of the interview booth wall. "Just give me the goddamn screwdriver and *you* hold this stupid piece of shit."

Jessie's massive presence grew closer, larger behind me.

"Why don't *I* hold the 'stupid piece of shit'? Kaitlin, I believe Paula has the updates to the software now. Why don't you help her set up her testing equipment?"

Kaitlin tried to keep me from glaring. She reminded me that it was not only unprofessional, but unfair. Demonstrating amazing restraint, I placed the side wall of the interview booth carefully into Jessie's waiting hands. Let him worry about lining up six screw holes the size of goddamn pin heads.

The boys' relief blew over me as I walked away.

On the other hand, Paula eyed me out of the corner of her eye.

"Do I need to get out my metal neck brace?"

Grimacing, I laughed.

"I think Gerard's jugular will hold me for a while. You should be safe. India and Andres got back with your changes pretty fast. Here, give me the box knife. Your stuff is in box three."

Paula handed me the knife. "How the heck do you remember that?"

"Useless trivia is my specialty."

I heaved the box onto the remaining conference table. Gerard had disassembled the conference table from the second room and propped its parts against the wall on this side of the room, leaving precious little space to work in over here. I sliced open the box and together we got to work on unwrapping the pieces and parts of her scanner.

Really, her scanner was just a mini, portable version of the interview booth. She used it to calibrate the software for the larger machine.

"I reread your report last night."

"All because you forgot one little statistic?"

"It was embarrassing. Anyway, I found another little statistic. One that gave me nightmares."

"And what was that?"

"That there are over 900 crew and staff on this boat."

"Ah," I looked down at the arrangement of camera parts we had created on the table. "You realize that is over 2,000 total permanent residents, including spouses and children?"

Paula froze in the process of screwing one of her three tiny cameras onto its tripod.

"Oh, god. I did not make that connection."

"Yeah."

"Just setting up for that many interviews would take six months."

"Well, they all have their mass transit IDs."

Paula waved that idea aside as she spread the legs on the final tripod. She set a workpad on a stand in front of me and locked her own pad into the privacy screen.

"Mass transit IDs are as easy to fake as drivers' licenses."

"Not that easy. And that part we can catch them at with a couple of extra cross checks."

Paula pursed her lips. "Maybe. I'll have to think about it. It's not my preference. I prefer being familiar with the data before I begin the interview."

In the chair across the corner from me, she settled down to bring the system online. Behind me I heard a crash and the whine of the power drill went silent.

"Who designed this fucking piece of shit anyway?" Gerard demanded.

"That would be you," I replied under my breath.

Paula just smiled.

My return smile was grim. That's right, banter, snarl, curse. Forget that the pole and the chair had vanished. Forget that shattered glass sprinkled the carpet next to my bed. Forget that a silk scarf lay pooled by the closet door. Forget that my body was so emotionally battered that just sitting in this chair made me ache.

"Okay," Paula said.

I looked up. Paula tilted her head, then shot me a woeful smile.

"Since you are in such a delightful mood this morning, I think we'd better take a few baseline scans before we get started."

I laughed despite myself. As the screen in front of me flickered to life, though, I started to wonder if I could handle more emotional manipulation so soon. That creeping feeling that started drilling up through my arms and legs told me no. The second I noticed it, I heard Ashley's fainting chant in the back of my head, "Let's get out of here. Gotta go. Let's get out of here. Gotta go...."

I jumped out of the chair.

"You know what? I'm always the one to sit for this. How are you ever going to know if that thing really works if it only tastes one brand of emotion every time? Gerard, since you are obviously incapable of handling a screwdriver, why don't you come sit for Paula this time? Take a little break."

Gerard jumped up from the floor and stretched his back.

"Hell, you wanna trade wrestling with Big Blue for sitting around pulling faces at stupid video clips, be my guest."

Just as I reached out to take the power drill from him, Jessie grabbed Gerard's shoulder.

"That's not how this works."

I saw, felt, the significant look pass between them. There was just enough of Stephan left in my head to see the faint image of Jessie trying to shut Gerard up and the barely there counter-image of Gerard wishing he'd kept his mouth shut. What the hell was that supposed to mean?

Kaitlin turned me around before anyone could recognize my reaction and dropped me back into the chair.

Paula sighed. I heard the faintest mutter, "...should put you all in time-out..." and then she resumed her preparations.

"Okay, for three of these tell me what you see. For one of them, lie to me."

I looked at the screen.

"I see a little knoll with the trunk of a fallen tree lying at the base of a pine and a...maybe a female elk tucked in the cranny they make."

Next picture.

"I see a rocky mountain, lots of moss, and a waterfall tumbling down the side of it."

"This is what I'm paying you guys the big bucks for?"

I looked up.

Cam.

He grinned. "Just thought I would see how the prisoners were doing."

He walked in, looking like sunshine, feeling like energy that had taken human form. That first layer of ache melted away from my flesh. Automatically, I rose in response and walked over to him.

"Come on in. We're still digging through boxes, but there's a few toys laying around that you might find interesting."

I drew him in through the narrow valley between the two tables. Ashley was so easy to ignore in that moment: it was as if she had vanished from me altogether.

Paula spared him a nod as he passed by, but Jessie and Gerard laid down their tools to greet him.

"Hey, you're Gerard O'Connell, right?"

The two men shook hands.

"That's right. Camden Glaswell?"

"Yes, sir. Good to meet you. And Jessie, how are you this afternoon?"

"Is it really afternoon already?"

"To the minute. So, what have we got here?"

I gestured to the mangled mass of plastic and metal. "We call this Plastics and Metals, Two. We thought it would make an elegant addition to your décor, welcoming guests in the check-in foyer when they first arrive on board."

Cam eyed it thoughtfully, then nodded.

"Stunning, truly stunning."

I laughed and caught Gerard's sidelong look at my abrupt change of humor. Screw him and his piece of crap cabin door security. Not fair, Kaitlin reminded me.

"It's the interview booth...eventually. Once we've got it together, it will have the body language sensors. That section over there," Jessie pointed to the blank console panel next in line for installation, "has all the vitals monitoring and then the facial cameras are in the upper side panels and that overhead panel over there." Jessie gestured to the curved sheet of metal studded with lights and lenses that I had propped in the corner to keep it from getting kicked.

In full presidential mode now, Jessie walked Cam back over to where Paula tapped at her workpad, probably resetting her baseline test.

"Paula, here, is working on the brains for the micro-expressions detector part of the booth. She just got some updates in and she's testing them. *Before* she inflicts them on the rest of us."

Cam grinned like a kid in the candy store, running his finger over the spherical case of one of Paula's cameras.

"So, can you try it on me?"

Paula smiled quietly.

"Not yet. This system will only check my suppositions against the database, so I can update it based on the test subject responses I collect. Once we get it installed in the booth, then you can lie to your heart's content."

"You be sure to call me. I want to be first in line to give that thing a try."

"Gonna try to beat the system?" Gerard asked.

"Wouldn't dream of it."

"Lie," Paula shot back.

Cam raised his eyebrows at her, then burst out laughing.

"I can see you guys sitting around the bar after work, telling these colossal stories and then everybody else sitting there say, 'Lie,' 'Truth,' 'Lie.' That's great."

Cam turned his joke toward me. That little extra light switched on in those eyes. That little extra pull in my stomach grew deeper, warmer. Kaitlin gave him a slow smile, then turned to Paula before it could get too obvious.

"Yeah, Paula, you're going to have to watch out for this guy," I warned her. "He's probably researched every lie detection countermeasure on the Internet."

"So, have I," she replied simply.

"Good, because I've briefed my security guys to give you a run for your money," Cam replied.

"Lie."

Cam threw his hands up. "Jesus! You watch out. My team recognizes a challenge when they hear it."

Jessie clapped a hand on Cam's shoulder.

"Go right on ahead. It's good to have someone keeping us on our toes. Now, weren't we supposed to be getting the schematics for this place pretty soon?"

Cam turned back to the three of us and a relieved Paula returned to her work. Paula was articulate enough and could hold her own during a presentation, but she very much preferred to leave the glad-handing to the rest of us.

"Oh. Yeah. J.C. asked me to tell you that he'll have that ready for you tomorrow. Not all the changes had been recorded to the master file and he wants to consolidate everything before he copies that over to you."

"Sounds fair enough. At this rate it looks like that's about when we'll be ready for it," Jessie replied looking around the room at the towers of equipment and supplies still needing to be unpacked.

And then there was that small matter of the three boxes of equipment that would have to be reordered.

Even as I looked around the mess for my workpad to do just that, Cam caught my gaze.

"Now, I was wondering if Kaitlin might have time to join me for lunch. Can you spare her for an hour or so?"

Cam was looking to Jessie for an answer, but it was Gerard who replied.

"Oh, you go right on ahead and take her. But you better make sure you've got all your shots updated first."

I shot him a look. "Thanks, Gerard."

Jessie went blank for a second, then his intention reached for me. He really didn't like the idea but picking through that lash of emotions so quickly made it hard for me to read why. A mess of anxiety, threads of anger, mistrust, surprise. But in seconds he had it back under control.

"I...I'll get my bag," I said.

Deliberately, I turned my back to Jessie, trying to give him at least the illusion of privacy. But there was a lingering little pain in my chest as I followed Cam out the door and I just couldn't be sure if it was my mentor's or if it was mine.

◆

"I'm going to pretend I'm not underdressed and covered with box dirt."

Cam pushed the door open ahead of me and we walked into Pioneer's Landing on a floor of the ship we couldn't even access without his ID.

"No one will notice."

I laughed. "You used to have a wife, you know how this works."

I caught the sharp lash of anger and hurt across the side of my body. I glanced over, felt him shake it off.

"You are nothing like my ex-wife. You could be covered with soot from head to foot and still walk through this place with your head up. You are absolutely nothing like her. But you won't need to worry about an audience for a couple weeks yet."

Ah, the elusive ex-wife. Never named. Never discussed except in brief references. But if it still hurt him that much, I guessed I could understand why.

I glanced around the glass and palm trees room and realized Cam was right about the audience. Only one table was occupied. When he headed for the balcony door, I hesitated. Midday at the equator wasn't my idea of comfortable. Cam caught my hesitation.

"Come on. It's not so bad. You'll see."

I shook my head and followed him out. As I passed through the door, I discovered that the balcony bore an almost completely transparent awning. A fine mist sifted down through the air, leaving the atmosphere sparkling and just cool enough to be comfortable. With a hand on my shoulder, Cam steered me to a green and glass table next to the balcony railing.

I bypassed the chair and leaned up against the railing overlooking the pool decks, several layers of the suite balconies, and the wide, white expanse of the elevator platform. To my left and right the sea went on for eternity, blending with the blue of the sky. I tossed my hair back and drank in the clean warmth of the sun, felt the mist soothe my skin.

"God, I needed this! This is gorgeous." I turned to look back at Cam. "Thank you."

The minute our eyes met, the radiant sunshine in him turned to a darker kind of heat. He stepped forward, brushed back a strand of hair that had caught on my lip.

"I missed you yesterday."

"Yeah."

My hand found its way to his shirt, my thumb ran circles over the center button. His hand stayed at my cheek, his thumb ran lines over my cheekbone. Maybe it was his intention that pulled me forward. Maybe I just stepped. If Ashley had any word of warning, I never heard it.

His breath came into me, filling my senses, my lungs with a sweet tang. His hand moved back to cradle my head as I let go and let him in. No more hesitation. My choice, my beautiful choice. His lips brushed mine, I rose up, wanting closer, wanting more. My hands found his hair, my body found his body. I felt him shudder as I pressed closer. The skin of his fingers wrapped around the naked flesh of my waist just under the tail of my shirt and kneaded and kneaded and kneaded until I groaned.

My back hit the railing. Cam pulled his lips away from mine with a ragged breath. I was already reaching for him, trying to pull him back.

"Kaitlin." He chuckled, very gently holding me still. "Oh, god. You are...I've been...oh, boy."

I pressed my cheek to his, just wanting to absorb one last bit of softness before I returned to reality.

Cam lifted his head. "Oh, look, it's starting."

Holding me close, he turned me around, wrapped his arms tight around me, rested his chin on my head. I registered his erection tucked between us and felt a strange combination of elation and chagrin.

Cam pointed out to the other end of the ship. I followed his gestured with my gaze. The elevator deck was moving!

"It's a test run of an actual canister car. This canister is just full of supplies for the space station, but it's the first run since the cable was completed two days ago."

My head still swayed. My body wanted to tremble against his body wrapped so tightly around me. I tried to remember how to focus.

"Two days ago?"

"Yeah, a full three weeks ahead of schedule."

"Slander and lies. Every contractor on the planet will see you hung."

"They aren't contractors. They're our own engineers."

"Oh."

He chuckled with his lips pressed into my hair.

"Here it comes."

The elevator platform was fully retracted now. The ship moaned and then shifted ever so slightly under our feet. A glass dome shaped like a bullet rose slowly into view, growing wider, then wider, then wider.

It had my attention now.

A band of metal, then more glass. Section, after section, after section. The two paddles became visible. No, not paddles. Those were the receiving panels for the lasers which powered the elevator. That was only the midway point.

"Oh, my god. It's huge!" I whispered.

"Just wait."

More sections. Up and up. Then a long, long swath of white-paneled hull. And finally, the space elevator came to a stop suspended just feet above the edge of the platform. Breathtakingly slowly, the platform rolled closed beneath it. The elevator ribbon was barely visible from where we stood. The long, elegant bullet appeared to dangle in mid-air.

"It looks like it's going to fall."

"Amazing isn't it?"

Now the panels rotated around the center of the machine. With precise movements, they aligned with the lasers below them. A slight jerk and they locked into place. Then, like a train, the elevator glided into motion, slowly, then faster, then faster—graceful, smooth, and impossible. Cam and I stood watching it until our eyes could no longer perceive its movement, until it just appeared to dangle forever between sea and sky.

"I never get tired of watching that."

I turned my head toward him. "Unbelievable. It was nothing like I expected."

Cam pulled me in tighter.

"Yeah, kind of like someone else I know."

I smiled and leaned back to rest my cheek against his shoulder. After a quick squeeze, he released me, gave my arms a brisk rub.

"Come on, I'd better feed you before I send you back or I have a feeling Jessie will have my hide."

He led me around to my chair and I took my seat.

"I'll be right back. I need to let Phil know we're out here."

I nodded. I could feel that familiar jitter in him ramping up as I watched him walk away. By the time he got back, his intention had shifted to a lashing, snapping swirl of mistrust and indecision. But it still reached for me. It still pulled.

I sighed.

"Tired?" he asked.

I sat up and pasted a smile on my face. Game time.

"A little." I leaned forward, tried to recapture some of that energy and fascination from just a moment before. "So, I have a question for you: Who goes? Up there."

"Just engineers, technicians. We're swapping out the crew a little—"

"No, I mean the settlers, the clients. You said that you never wanted for investors. Who is it who's so desperate to run away? What is so awful that they would take such a huge risk?"

I looked up to the heavens where the elevator had become entangled with a low-lying cloud. I felt a subtle change in his intention, a slight softening.

"Run away," he repeated.

I kept my eyes turned away, but that softening tugged at me. The door to Ashley's closet slipped open. She wandered out into my mind as I spoke.

"It's so dangerous. They have everything to lose. They will never see or hear from their friends and family again. They may get there and find their assigned planet totally uninhabitable. They may never even survive the voyage and if they do, just the physical and mental hardships of establishing the settlement...I can't even imagine. But you say you've never lacked for investors." But I was starting to see it, starting to understand. Because maybe I was starting to understand just what it was to feel that hopeless and terrified, like there were simply no choices left.

"Some of them are desperate," Cam replied slowly. "But...for most it is a leap of faith."

I looked down at my place setting, trying to coax Ashley back into the darkness, but I was too emotionally off balance.

"Like Will's Pilgrims and their comets?"

Cam was watching me far too closely; his hand reached for mine across the slightly slick glass table top. He played his thumb over my knuckles.

"Yeah, that's a fair comparison. We even get our fair share of religious groups looking to create their own promised land. But whatever brings them here, Will demands complete honesty with regards to the chances of success. And the Pilgrims themselves knew what they were getting into. There had been no successful settlement before them. Will tosses out some pretty scary statistics on the most famous one, Jamestown. The original settlement had 108 people. 38 survived the first year. Then they built it up to 500. Only 60 survived the winter. The Pilgrims knew that, but they packed up their wives and children and went anyway. Without the leap of faith, how desperate do you think they would have had to be?"

I shook my head, mesmerized by the movement of his hand.

"More desperate than me."

His intention went still, the only sound the breeze through the potted palm behind him.

"Have you...have you ever been that desperate, Kaitlin?"

A memory slipped through: kissing my unknowing mother goodbye for the last time, her beautiful brown eyes so happy to see me. God, I missed her so much it hurt.

But I smiled at the table, tilted my head up to him.

"How 'bout you? Have you ever been that desperate, Cam?"

Cam gave my hand a squeeze.

"Secrets, Kaitlin. Secrets."

Then he pulled his hand away.

◆

It was irresponsible of me, but I meandered my way back to our makeshift office. I strolled through the packed food court and tried to untangle my brain.

Secrets.

What would the Director of Port Security do with my secrets? So impossible to separate the man from the job. Who was I kidding chasing after a relationship with Camden Glaswell? Where the hell could it possibly go?

Nowhere, Ashley whispered, *nowhere at all.*

I looked at the crowd, picked out a family settling in over baskets of overstuffed sandwiches. I watched them. The boy flicked a pickle at his little sister. The dad laughed; the mother scolded. The sister retaliated with tiny handful of lettuce. I hadn't felt so alone since my flight cross country from Seattle to Miami—like a wall, a huge wall of secrets stood between me and the rest of humanity. But how was I ever going to change that?

Blankly, I turned away, turned down the empty hallway and headed for the elevator.

"Where do you think you're going?"

A hand closed over my arm, tried to drag me into the employee entrance for the Chinese food stand. I jerked back, found myself face to face with Mak.

Oh, shit.

"I don't give a fuck what you did to Stephan..." He got me by both arms and shoved me against the doorframe. "...you are going to give us those blueprints or I am going to show up in your room in the middle of the goddamn fucking night and slit your goddamn throat!"

He rammed his forearm against my throat and flipped open a nasty serrated knife just at the periphery of my vision.

"Got that, you worthless little cunt?"

His rage beat into me until my own head roared with it; the sight of that knife left my mind numb.

"I—" I coughed against the choking pressure of his arm. He shifted his clenched fist from my arm to my hair, yanking my head back and leaving my neck exposed.

He wanted so badly to kill me right there. He hated me that much. Why? I had to give him something. I had to interrupt his train of thought.

I scrambled to grab my mini from my pocket.

"I don't have them—"

"Don't give me that, bitch."

The knife bit into my neck. My knees came loose. He wasn't strong enough to hold me up like that. I started to slide down the wall.

"Yet. Yet. Tomorrow."

Mak saw the mini in my hand. He grabbed it from me and threw it across the hall.

"The meeting schedule. It's on..."

I clutched weakly at his arm. Abruptly, he released me, disappeared through the doorway. With the pressure gone, I lost myself in a violent coughing fit.

"Miss, are you alright? Do you need some water?"

I glanced over, saw a woman's black flats. I nodded to her, keeping my hair down over the welts on my neck. But through the tears and the pain, Kaitlin smiled a feral smile. The woman walked away to get my water. I raised my head, crossed the hall, and gingerly retrieved my discarded mini.

Fingerprints.

Now who's the worthless cunt, jackass?

12

"Fingerprints?" Jessie eyed my mini suspiciously. Then he looked at my neck. "Do I even want to know how you got them?"

"I'm saving the nervous breakdown for later."

"You are bleeding."

"Like I said: Later."

Jessie was very, very quiet for a very, very long time. His mind, not so much. Waves of protectiveness pulled at my shoulders, trying to draw me closer. Watchful anger radiated out through the narrow space. And fear. Fear nearly strong enough to take shape without Stephan's help penetrated through me each time his gaze flicked over to the trickle of blood on my neck.

I looked up and down the hallway, trying to give him space. Inside me, Ashley pounded against her door like some kind of enraged chimpanzee. Kaitlin simply stood quietly, ready for the next move.

"They want the schematics."

Jessie's eyebrows rose. "Wasn't your Stephan some kind of small-time burglar? What do they want with the ship's schematics?"

"I don't know. Maybe that's what they're here to steal."

It was possible, I realized, that it was just that simple. Those schematics were so tightly guarded that we hadn't even been allowed a copy during the bidding process.

"Your face is saying 'but.'"

I shook my head.

"It doesn't feel right. They've dug in here. They're taking their time setting me up. They're here to do something more than just lift some architectural drawings. They've got to be."

"It's not your job to find out what that is, Osgood. Are we clear?"

Already I could feel my fingers starting to shake. I let out a short laugh.

"Don't worry. I don't think I'm cut out to be a secret agent."

"I'll see what I can do about getting the prints off this. I'll send it over to you, so you can ID the guy. This is your Mak, right? The one with the criminal record?"

I nodded.

"But once you confirm the ID, this goes straight to Cam. Got it?"

"Yes, sir."

"Now go have your nervous breakdown," he ordered gesturing down the hall to the ladies' room.

I'd intended to protest, but I heard the tremor in my laugh.

"Yes, sir."

◆

It was a swap.

In the dim lamplight, I stared at the picture of Maxwell McKinnis on my workpad screen. Age 22. Residence: Seattle, Washington. The only reason this kid had a file was because he had participated in his elementary school fingerprinting program.

Shit. So much for my career as a secret agent.

It wasn't a half bad swap. The kid did look a little like Mak. The names were similar. The age was way off, but the average interviewer might not notice that. More importantly, what the average interviewer would never notice was the way this kid's eyes were capable of gentle happiness. Endless years of anger had etched lines around Mak's eyes that would never disappear completely, not even in sleep.

Hate.

He hated me enough to want to kill me. Not casually, but personally. He actually wanted me dead.

Why?

Because of the girl from the botched burglary? Because of Stephan? I had a feeling the reasons would only make sense to Mak, even if I knew them.

I raised my fingers to the cut just below the juncture of my jawbone and my ear. It burned and tore just the tiniest bit with the movement.

...you are going to give us those blueprints or I am going to show up in your room in the middle of the goddamn fucking night and slit your goddamn throat!

My heart tripped in my chest and I gripped my workpad tighter. I needed a new strategy. This file alone would not be enough to remove him from public life, from my life.

I set the workpad on the nightstand, switched out the light, and brought the rough-satiny comforter up to my chin. I stared out into the darkness.

I don't give a fuck what you did to Stephan...

My bark of laughter echoed around the room, sending a shiver chasing across my ribs. What *I* did to Stephan? What *I* did to Stephan? My gaze dropped to the shadows at the foot of my bed. I saw his dark eyes widen, his mouth go loose in shock.

You left because of me. You are...you are terrified of me.

I covered my face with my hands, but the image of him only grew clearer.

I can't leave you like this. God, please don't hate me.

I scrambled out of bed, kicking frantically at the sheets which grabbed at my ankles. For a second, I just clutched at my arms, pacing back and forth alongside the bed. He'd switched me off like a fucking light!

And me sitting here in the same room, in the same exposed position, because switching rooms would be a pointless exercise, a futile gesture that would send red flags to Cam, but more importantly to Stephan and Mak. Like getting on the intercom and shouting that they were winning, that I was scared, and I was running. That after all their demonstrations, I was still stupid enough to think they couldn't get to me anywhere, anytime.

So here I was looking at the red circles I'd painted around myself. Alone, because I would never, ever use Jessie as a human shield.

Stupid, so stupid. But dealing with whatever they decided to do to me was one thing. Surviving if they went through Jessie to get to me, that I could never do.

I fisted my hands in my hair.

Wildly, I broke out of my pacing and jogged over to the love seat, yanked the cushions free. Tucking them under one arm, I pulled the comforter from the bed, used my last free fingers to snag a pillow. I rammed the fluffy mass through the bathroom doorway. After an awkward struggle, I managed to get the door closed. With my feet, I shoved the cushions up against the door. The blanket and pillow came down with me, creating a lumpy, too small nest.

I pushed my back up against that flimsy door and some of the tension released from my body. Good thoughts, Kaitlin ordered. Carefully, I took deliberate control of my breathing. Slow down.

Good thoughts.

Cam's arms around me. Watching the elevator vanish from view. Cam's lips on mine, his hands on my skin. The feeling of coming beautifully undone. His breath filling me. His vibrant energy washing away all that terrible pain. Those brilliant penetrating eyes watching me so carefully, knowing...something.

"Secrets, Kaitlin. Secrets."

In that place between sleeping and waking, I whimpered.

13

I was the first to spot J.C., the Port Operations Manager, peering in the door.

Of course, my eye had almost never turned from that mark since I'd arrived in our temporary office two hours ago. I saw his gaze go to the disassembled conference table. I caught the little punch of displeasure. Trust Gerard not to ask before he took his power drill to something.

But when J.C. caught sight of what we had built in its stead, I felt his desire to check out the shiny new gadgets quickly overcome his annoyance. I waved him over.

The four of us were just completing setup on two workstations—giant workpads on stilts. J.C. grinned at Jessie sitting cross-legged on the floor and pushed his thinning hair back from his eyes.

"Now that's what I like to see. Think I could get Will to lend a hand every once in a while down at the canister facility? That would be a picture."

Jessie waved a hand at me.

"Blame her. Slave driver."

"He tried to convince me that it was far more presidential to be compiling reports and budget statistics poolside," I acknowledged.

Paula actually tossed her head back in laughter.

Jessie shot her one of his rare smiles.

"Hey, I can be presidential."

Paula blushed, but she was still chuckling as she returned to strapping the wiring to the leg of the work station.

"Monitoring stations?" J.C. asked.

I nodded. "This one is for the queue and this one is for the interview room. We'll be—"

"Which are completely freaking useless without my damn cameras," Gerard griped, standing up from behind Big Blue.

"Your cameras are coming, Gerard. Probably by Friday of next week," I reminded him.

"You know, I probably have a couple I can spare if you'll put my *damn* table back together. Maybe next time you could call me and I'd have a couple of facilities guys come take it away instead of dismembering it."

"Yeah, Gerard," Jessie muttered from underneath the station.

Gerard threw his hands up, drill and all. "Hey, I'm not a 'have your people call my people' kinda guy. Now if one of you suits had been around when you were supposed to be..."

I turned to J.C. "What Gerard is trying to say is that he would be happy to reassemble your table and that I will give you a call when it is ready to be picked up."

"Thank you. Now Cam said you were looking for this." He held up a black plastic stick, the old-fashioned kind complete with USB jack.

Gerard immediately grabbed it.

"Finally! Now I can finally stop being everybody else's grease monkey and start doing some real work."

Even without seeing his intention incarnate, J.C.'s desire to grab that stick back from Gerard's apparently untrustworthy hands came through loud and clear. Kaitlin reminded me to keep my smile to myself.

I held my hand out for the stick and with a roll of his eyes, Gerard turned it over.

"Now you realize this is a your-eyes-only file. If you try to transmit it, it will erase. If you try to take it off the ship, it will erase. This file is worth millions on the black market. Only myself, Cam, the captain, and the chief engineer have access to it. Oh, and Will, of course."

The file went from feeling like a stick of cold plastic to feeling like a stick of hot dynamite in my palm. I raised my eyebrows.

"But what about the rest of the security team: Davina and Arlen and those people? Don't they need this information to do their jobs?"

"They have their maps. You don't need this level of information to schedule security patrols. Now, if anything should happen—if you even suspect you just misplaced it—contact me immediately, so I can remotely erase it. Understood?"

"Understood, sir," Jessie replied. "Do you have time to give us a quick walk through, so we can be prepared for the tour?"

J.C. glanced at his mini, then slid it back in his pocket. "Yeah, I have a few seconds."

I got the impression he meant that literally. I got Paula up with a jerk of my head.

"The projector is in Kaitlin, Box 1. You still have the box knife?"

She pulled it out and came with me to help. Fortunately, the projector was in the upper layers of filler.

We cleared a space on the unvandalized conference table. I plugged the stick into the small pad and turned it on. After a few bits of instruction, a transparent ship built of blue lines sprang to life above the table.

J.C. stepped forward.

"Alright. Operations starts about here," he said, pointing just forward of mid-ship. He moved his finger backward from there. "The spare elevator is here. The elevator bay is here."

J.C. move himself out of the way and gestured to a large empty area near the end of the ship. "Canisters are assembled all the way back here toward rear of the ship. The first stop they make is here at the canister loading facility where all the non-human cargo is added—all the equipment the settlers will need, agricultural and otherwise, to get started. Then the canister rolls forward to the cryogenics lab where the settlers' containers will be installed. After that the canisters slide forward and are fitted into the lower portion of the next available elevator. This area above is for the boarding of the elevator's regular passengers and crew members, loading of space station supplies.

"Other than that, there are security stations at both entrances to operations here and here." He gestured vaguely to the fifth-floor check points we were all familiar with. "And this entire rear section of the ship is dedicated to engineering."

I stared through those blue lines. What in the hell were Stephan and Mak here to steal?

"...to go. Kaitlin. Kaitlin?"

"Kaitlin."

I jerked my head around at the touch of Jessie's hand on my shoulder.

"J.C. needs to leave."

"Oh, thanks for this, J.C. This'll be great."

J.C. just gave me a distracted nod as he walked out the door, head already bent over his workpad.

Neither Paula, nor Jessie, not even Gerard said a word as I pulled a chair over and started taking the schematics apart, level by level, room by room.

What was here that I wasn't seeing? What take was so incredible that it could unite two archenemies for a heist this delicate?

Come on out, Ashley. Tell me what the hell it is that I'm not seeing.

◆

"Break time."

I jumped straight out of my chair, spun around, and caught Jessie's hand where it had sat on my shoulder. A violent re-entry into reality.

My brain was full of giant rails, canisters, plows, seeds, and chickens caught in suspended animation. And a serrated blade at the corner of my vision that never stopped moving.

Jessie extricated his hand from my grip. He reached past me and powered down the projector.

"Time to hit the gym."

"Oh, um, yeah."

He pulled the chair aside and I walked around it. Gerard and Paula were already waiting at the door. I grabbed my bag and hurried after them. We stood around and waited while Jessie used his ship ID to lock the door.

Beside me, a softness drifted from Paula. Stealing a glance, I saw her watching Jessie's hands with the sweetest look in her eyes. Before he could turn around, it was gone—as was that gentle pull.

I averted my gaze in surprise. Was that new? How had I missed that? And then I thought of those countless hours I'd spent sitting across from her staring into those cameras.

Oh, god. I hadn't missed that. She was hiding it from me. She believed. She actually believed. Out of the three people around whom my world revolved, the one so carefully kept in the dark was the one who believed in my freakish little ability. My stomach gave a little lurch.

Paula knew what I could do.

Now veterans of the locker-less gym, we detoured first to the restrooms down the hall from our office. That flutter in my center followed me all the way inside. Dropping my bag, I leaned back against the door.

"Paula."

She turned, looked back at me with her eyebrows wrinkled in puzzlement.

"I..." I looked around the utilitarian white tiled room. How the hell did I broach this? I'd never done it before. "I felt you. You don't have to hold back from Jessie like that. You'd be good for him. He's lonely."

Paula's intentions became a definite shove.

"That was private, Kaitlin."

I blushed. "I know. I, um, I don't usually, I mean I try not to, but I would feel so bad if..." I sighed. This was not going well.

The shove slackened, and Paula just shook her head.

"It doesn't matter, Kaitlin. He's already built himself the perfect woman." She gestured at me. "Perfect hair, perfect face, perfect body. Perfect social graces. Perfectly unattainable." She sighed. "It really doesn't matter."

I stared at her, a pained sort of laugh pushing out from between my lips.

"Me? No, Jessie and me? That would be...that would just be wrong."

"Exactly and that's exactly how he wants it. If you stay unattainable, then you stay perfect. And he has absolutely no need for someone like me."

"Paula."

Her smile was so sad I felt my heart breaking, even as I absorbed her pain.

"I can't do what you do, but I have my databases and I have my eyes."

"You wouldn't even consider giving him a chance to change his mind? I don't have your brain, but I know what I feel and 'afar' isn't working for him." I wasn't sure I believed what she was saying, but her twisting, penetrating ache killed me.

Paula pressed her lips together. She started to answer me, but then the tears started.

"I...I think maybe I'd better go. You can tell them...tell them..."

I pulled her in for a quick hug, felt those tiny, fragile bones in my arms.

"Go, before they get out. I'll just tell them you weren't feeling well."

Her satin head nodded into my shoulder. Keeping her face down, she hurried from the restroom.

Alone, I blinked back tears of my own. I felt disoriented, her pain lingering with me long after she was gone.

Could she be right?

Or was that just her fear talking?

The thing with brilliant people was they could come up with equally brilliant reasoning for whatever path they chose to take—right or wrong.

I remembered Jessie's reaction when Cam came to take me to lunch. But shouldn't he feel *something* when someone showed up intending to usurp his role? Platonic or not, we'd had only each other for so long.

Had I been oblivious? I shook out my head and reached for my gym clothes.

Planting seeds could be so dangerous.

But I knew one flaw in her theory upfront. Only to her could I possibly appear perfect. Jessie, and only Jessie, knew exactly how imperfect I really was.

As I pulled on my workout gear, that already distracting question was joined by another:

Just how long had she believed?

◆

When we returned from the workout, I shifted from the ship's schematics to one of the workstations. Ashley had been no help at all with determining what Stephan and his people might plan to steal. Escape routes, hidey holes, sure, but nothing about what Pioneers' Port's crown jewels might be. To be fair, Ashley's role in Stephan's gang had primarily been lookout. When she—when I—willingly joined with Stephan not only did it gift intentions with their own incarnations, but it also massively expanded my range from a few feet to roughly a half-block radius. Overwhelming for me, but incredibly useful for a band of mid-list thieves.

I began by pulling up all the news I could find about Pioneer's Port itself. There was a lot. Too much. I sorted and categorized. Tried to look for reoccurring names. The most prominent topic was controversy over the program itself. The same things I'd wondered about—was it thinly veiled suicide being sold to the desperate and delusional?

I tapped at the screen, staring at the article. Still nothing to steal. I kept flipping.

"Hey, it's getting late. Why don't you walk back with us?"

I waved Jessie off, not even looking over my shoulder.

"I've got to figure this out. I know it's obvious. I've got to be on the right track."

"I don't like the idea of you walking back alone."

I kept flipping through the articles on the giant workpad. I forgot to answer him, never heard them leave.

14

"No!"

"Whoa, it's just me."

I jerked upright, blinking to clear my eyes. Cam stood beside me, one hand on my shoulder, one hand carrying a white fast food bag. I shuddered, then slumped over, pressing my hands to my face. Cam's humor and concern wrapped around me.

He rubbed my back, chuckling.

"*Shooting Felons to the Stars: A Second Chance or Just the Latest Form of Guilt-Free Execution?* Yeah, falling asleep reading that would give me nightmares, too."

Groaning, I raised my face from my hands. After a couple of tries, my mouth finally engaged.

"Is this for real?"

Cam laughed. "Oh, it's real. Probably about fifty percent of our clientele are countries unburdening their penal systems."

"Wow."

"It's not exactly a new practice. Britain used to offload its convicts to colonies in the U.S., Australia, and India. Even parts of the Galapagos Islands you just came from used to be a penal colony."

I rubbed at the squished side of my face, then reached out and powered the monitoring station down.

"And these guys, are they taking your leap of faith, too?"

"Will won't take them unless they've signed off that they are making the choice of their own free will. In some countries that still doesn't mean much, but it's the best we can do for now."

Cam raised the bag. "Jessie told me to drag you out of here and feed you. Come on. Let's go trail shredded lettuce down the promenade. Really piss off Lou and Xiaomei."

Jessie told him? What on earth did that mean? Ashley sank her hooks right into that one. I shook her off. Didn't matter. Right now, it really didn't matter. With a smile, I hopped down from the stool. Now that the spare table was gone, we could actually walk side by side out of the room. I snagged my bag on the way out.

"Do you really know the name of everyone who works here?"

"I try. Best way to keep the peace."

We waved goodnight to Dmitri at the security check point. Ashley always got so agitated every time we passed through the simple metal detector. Kaitlin just smiled at the well-rounded officer. He smoothed the sides of his mustache sternly.

"You two should be outside watching that sunset. You spend too much time inside. It is not good for your health. Out, out with you."

People, Kaitlin reminded Ashley. *Just people.*

Ashley shook her head. *Fake. Trying to trick you into trusting them. Stay away.*

This time, I was the one to slide Ashley back into her closet. I didn't like her talking about Dmitri that way, not when I could feel his conflicting desires for company and for our happiness playing tenderly back and forth. I gave his arm a squeeze as I passed by.

Cam called over his shoulder.

"Yeah, we all know who *really* runs this place!"

"Fresh air, director. She should not be so pale in your care."

I blinked. *In your care?*

Cam caught my look of surprise.

"Village gossip is the primary form of entertainment around here."

Ashley made a desperate play to lock my legs. I breathed through her anxiety. *If Dmitri has heard, then Stephan will hear.*

Breathe.

"You okay?"

"Yeah, just forgot we had an audience, I guess."

"It's mostly harmless." Cam dropped back and settled his arm across my back, his hand on my shoulder. His intention pulled me in before his body did. All that heat spreading through me, from his body, from his mind, melted away the last of Ashley's hold. I raised my arm to his waist and pressed my head to his shoulder.

In that moment I didn't even care if we'd just given Dmitri a little something to take back to the gossip mill.

In that moment my world was perfect.

◆

"Dmitri wasn't kidding about the sunset."

The half-sun that remained painted the sky in golds, blues, and blacks. Cam relaxed against the railing beside me, one hand kneading the muscles in my neck until I wanted to purr.

"I actually can't remember the last time I stood and watched the sun go down," I agreed.

I leaned out over the railing. The breeze blew my hair back as I looked down at the white water shoved aside by the immensity of this floating city. The captain and his team were maneuvering the ship in a precise pattern that would relocate the space station out of the flight path of a satellite without causing excessive whiplash for the occupants of the station or for the crew of the elevator.

I straightened and turned my face upward, trying to picture the movement of the ribbon, the elevator, the space station. I shook my head.

"Amazing."

The warmth of Cam's palm closed over the side of my neck, his cool fingertips pressed into the divot of my spine. He gave a little tug and I turned to face him, my heart in my throat. I looked up into those eyes, more electric than the painting of the sun; those soft lashes promising gentle, sweet sensations I didn't have names for. My chest grew tight and I shivered.

"Come with me."

His hand lowered down my arm to my hand. His other hand relieved me of my bag.

"This way."

The wooden deck rang loud with each step we took in our tidy business shoes. I wanted to kick them off and float like I was supposed to, along with the breeze. I followed him up a flight of metal stairs, across a second deck. He held the door open for me as we re-entered the ship. As the door closed behind us the air in the hallway grew distressingly still. I wanted to float.

Instead, I stroked his hand with my thumb as he pulled me forward, his intention stuttering between the ghostly hands that roamed over my body and his hesitation, dark and confused. I tried to keep my reactions from my face as I struggled to breathe.

We reached his door and he unlocked and opened it one-handed, as if he was afraid to release me. He dropped my bag beside the door, drew me inside. The door closed behind us both with an unsettling click.

His apartment.

In the half-light from the balcony window across the living room, Cam studied my face. He was so painfully torn. Secrets. My secrets.

His hands ran up my arms, buried themselves in my hair.

"Tell me, Kaitlin. Please just tell me."

So hard to breathe. I strained forward against his grip, tilting my face up toward his, my breasts so achingly heavy.

"Davina hates you and Will. Will is alarmingly genuine. Arlen wants to fuck me."

Cam gave my head a shake.

"Kaitlin!"

"You...you don't want to want me, but..." I sank my teeth into my lip, trying to bite back a groan. "...but you already have my breasts in your hands."

"Kaitlin." This time it was a hoarse whisper. He laid his temple against mine. My breath hitched in his ear and he trembled. "Can't you just trust me?"

"Can't *you* trust *me*?" I begged. I felt the barest touch of the corner of his lips against mine. I lunged.

Our teeth tapped our mouths came together so hard. His tongue thrust between my lips and he drilled down so far into me I felt my center tighten convulsively. I cried out, my shaking hands clawing at his arms. He raked his hands down my hair, found the shoulders of my wide-neck silken T-shirt and yanked. I heard seams pop, fabric tear. My breasts sprang free, but the neckline bound my elbows to my sides with a cutting tension.

"You said I've got your breasts in my hands."

"Oh, god. Cam!"

He wrapped a hand around the base of each breast and shook them until the heat was unbearable. I begged wordlessly, but he merely backed me into the living room. I hit the back of the couch and he leaned me back over it until everything I was became that unrelieved ache, throbbing into the points of my nipples.

Abruptly, he slowed. He tugged the shirt and bra lower until I was pinned at the wrists, but he had full access to my torso. As I writhed, he stroked his palms over my skin, dipping in for a teasing lick at first one, then the other nipple. Then his hands moved lower, closed over the belt to my slacks. I bucked. He clamped his mouth over my left breast and sucked, hard. I screamed.

The pants, the panties scraped down my hips, down my legs. Even from this awkward position my hips thrust and my head thrashed wildly. We pulled my feet free from the shoes and I kicked the rest away.

He grabbed me by the arm and pulled me upright. I tugged and yanked and finally got my wrists free of the shirt. I drove my fingers into his hair, a silky glide that ended too soon. I nipped at his lower lip, wanting more, wanting to take all of him and wrap him around me, pull him inside me, absorb everything about him.

Cool fingers traced the too hot flesh of my waist. He managed to unhook the bra. I heard more fabric tear as he drew the shirt down over my ass and let it pool around my feet. He pulled his face back, looked down at me. The golden last-light played over his features. His eyes softened and the fire and frenzy in him gentled its hold on me, gentled me. I trembled under his hands. I wanted that. I wanted that to be mine. Was that so wrong?

"Kaitlin."

Was that even my name?

He raised his hands to my face, swept his thumb over my cheekbone, leaving a cool, moist line. I lifted a startled hand to my cheek. Tears?

Cam pulled me in, wrapped his arms around my nakedness. His cold, crisp shirt pressed against my burning breasts; the chill of his belt buckle dug into my navel; the hot, hard length of his penis pulled at my answering heat. I knew how desperately he wanted to drive himself inside me. Instead he pressed a simple, sweet kiss to my forehead.

"Come with me."

He took me by the hand and led me away from the living room. I walked, a little anxious, a little lost following behind him with my bare breasts swaying, him still in full business attire. I kept my mind carefully blank as I looked up at his lean, square shoulders. No. No Kaitlin, no Ashley. Just me. Just him.

His room was nearly the same as mine, same bed, same lamp, same mirrored closet. Only the dimensions were slightly larger. He drew me to a stop next to the bed. In front of the mirrored closet.

"Look."

He turned me around to face the mirror. I hesitated, offering the slightest resistance to his gentle push. That face, that body wasn't me. But he turned my head back and I relented. He ran his hands up, up through my hair until I straightened my posture. He stroked his hands up my neck until it was long and regal. He reshaped my shoulders, lifted my breasts as if offering myself to me, piece by piece. He worked his way down past my butt, my thighs, my calves, even my feet, as if to say, *This is you, right here. This is you.*

I tottered as he lowered my last foot to the floor. He caught me around the thighs, placed a kiss on my hip. As he rose, I slid my hand down over the front of his pants, closed it around what he was denying us both. He jerked at my touch and his forehead pressed into my shoulder. I reached behind me and pulled him closer in. As his pulsing length seated itself in the cleft of my ass, he groaned.

Impatient, I let myself fall forward over the edge of the bed and matched us the way we were supposed to be.

"Please, now," I whimpered.

His intention already had me spread wide, filled utterly. When I heard the clank of his belt buckle, I moaned, arching my hips. *Now, now, now!*

A new sensation, hot, smooth, heavy. We sought each other, found each other. One thrust, two thrusts. Complete. His fingers dug into my hips as he held me motionless. I grabbed handfuls of the comforter, shoved it in my face to muffle my screams. I tossed my head, felt my hair feather over my back.

Then finally, finally, finally he began to move. I clutched at the blankets, clutched at anything. My shoulders dug into the mattress; my breasts slapped the side of the bed. I raised my head to cry out and saw him watching us in the mirror. Him, clothed and controlled; me, naked and wild.

I didn't care.

He nudged me up on the bed. Then he dug his hands into my hair and rode me. My screams turned into sobs. He reached under me, first to grip my breasts, and knead and pull and flick at too-hard nipples. Then his fingers moved lower, gliding so close to where I was coming apart, so close to where I was losing myself. His fingertips burrowed in, between the folds, a single slide of callused skin against moist, tender flesh.

"Oh, god! Oh, god!"

My body pulled apart from inside, my mind flew open into emptiness. Cam grabbed my hips and pounded us together, so fast; my body going limp, my mind gone.

I heard his guttural cry, felt the jerk and the heat.

We collapsed together in the knot of icy metallic sheets.

◆

I've got the gun again. It's like poison in my hand. My fingers, my palm grow itchy, achy. I look down and see my skin turning black. That girl, Mak's girl sits in front of me, her blood pooling around her, soaking her clothes. She fades slowly, like some macabre Cheshire Cat, until all that is visible are those terrified eyes, that creeping pool of blood.

"No! Please, I'll get help. Don't!"

Like before, Amilee and Stephan come thundering down the stairs, the sound deafening to my ears. They strip the gun from my blackened arms. I try to run to the place where the girl should be. Amilee and Stephan pin me in place.

I hear the front door open. I see Mak walk around the corner, stare down at those eyes, the blood.

"You killed her."

"No, Stephan says she's alright. He says it's scratches...the wood."

Mak raises his pant leg, draws a knife from a sheath around his calf. He advances on me as flames ripple and shoot around him. The whole house is on fire except for the place where I stand, where Amilee and Stephan hold me fast.

Amilee strokes my hair back from my face and presses her cheek to my head.

"We'll always be best friends. I'll never leave you."

Mak steps closer, but I can't get my arms free. Amilee and Stephan don't even seem to see him at all. Him or the flames that creep forward with him.

Stephan's lips lower to my ear. His free hand caresses my breast, shaping, lifting the tender flesh.

"I love you, Ashley. Do you think you'll ever find another soulmate? Do you think you'll ever find what we have with someone else? Love me, Ashley." His hand slides lower, grips me, abruptly, harshly between the legs. "Ashley, you're mine. Every part of you will always be mine."

"No!"

Mak stands directly in front of me now, the wind from his flames whipping at my face, tearing at my hair, my clothes. My two friends hold me for him, presenting me to his knife. The tip reaches for the flesh of my neck.

"Oh, god!"

I buck, kick out with both feet. Somehow, somehow, I break free, land hard on my back on the stairs. Mak's fire is burning my feet. I scream.

Desperately, I twist around. The three of them grab for me as I scramble on all fours up the stairs, their nails raking into the flesh of my calves. The edges of the wooden steps crack against my shins, dig into my palms. I've got to move faster. I can feel the blood trickling down the backs of my legs.

I launch myself toward the first landing.

It isn't there.

There is nothing.

Pure, perfect, frozen darkness.

I can't breathe. I flail against the emptiness.

"Ssh, hey. It's okay. Hey, breathe."

Somewhere, from out of the darkness, warmth reaches out for me. I clutch after it, burrow into it. I'm trembling from the cold, the pain, the fear. The warmth wraps around me, pulls me tight, holds me safe.

The tremors loosen their hold on me, leak out of my body, down my cheeks...away.

Peace slowly seeps in.

Peace and a dreamless sleep.

15

I blinked, surprised to find myself waking, surprised to find myself so relaxed in an actual bed. I raised my head just enough to see the clock on the wallpad.

11:52 p.m.

Silently, I groaned.

An arm and a leg had my body pinned to the bed; a twist of sheets covered my lower back and ankles. I shivered in the chill. That arm moved; the big hand rubbed soothing circles over my naked back.

"Ssh," a sleeping voice whispered.

A sweet ache filled my chest as I drank in that unconscious tenderness. Despite the cold, I didn't want to move, didn't even want to twitch if it might break this perfect moment.

11:53 p.m.

I had to go. Cam worked here, and he didn't need rumors about some contractor with a torn shirt and sex hair walking out of his apartment in the wee hours of the morning. I sighed quietly.

Carefully, I started to slide away. That arm and leg caught me, pulled me in.

I gave a startled laugh.

"Where you goin'?" Sleep slurred his speech, left his body warm and languid against mine. Languid and naked as the soft, sweet press of his penis against my thigh told me. Smiling, I twined my limbs with his, pressed the fullness of my breasts against his solid chest.

"Trying to preserve your honor."

"Mmm."

He rolled over on top of me. He spread my legs with his knees, leaving me exposed to the cold air, his penis dangling tantalizingly close. The weight of him crushed the air from my chest, turning my breath into short, quick gasps. He nuzzled my neck. I could already feel my center tightening. I moaned and shifted my hips.

As his teeth and tongue sent tiny, electric tremors through me, I ran my hands over him, exploring everything I'd missed the first time. Cam wasn't intimidatingly muscular like Jessie and Gerard. The muscles under my hands were solid, sleek, strong. I slid my hands down to his buttocks, massaged until he groaned into my ear, then tilted him down toward me, toward my building ache. I felt him twitch against me.

Giving his shoulder a shove, I rolled us over.

With one hand planted in the pillow beside his head, I reached down between us and coaxed him back to wakefulness. The strength of him lifted, shoved against me. I guided him home.

"Oh, god! You don't mess around, do you!"

I chuckled as he grabbed my hips, forcing me to a slower rhythm.

For a second, I bit at my lower lip, waiting for the pain to subside.

"You okay?" he murmured, eyes still closed.

"Yeah, just been a while."

"A while?"

"'Bout four years."

"Jeezus!"

Laughing, I clamped down around him, tired of waiting, tired of letting him have all the control. He jerked. On a gut deep groan, I stretched, reached out for the headboard, shifting the angle. With an explosive breath his eyes popped open. For a second, he watched my breasts dance over him. I shuddered as his intention suckled and nipped. His head raised, but he couldn't reach me. His hands jumped from my hips to my breasts. Clutching me hard, he raised up his hips and rammed into me, harder, faster. I was screaming again.

He flipped me over so hard my head bounced against the mattress. He attacked my left breast, drawing it in. Using suction and the back of his tongue he rolled my nipple against the roof of his mouth. His thumb and his forefinger lifted the weight of my right breast by the nipple alone. All the while he pounded into me, sliding me forward, pinning my head back as my hair got caught underneath us.

I opened my legs wider. He pushed them wider still. I was going to crack open. He released my breasts, drove his thumbs down and opened me up.

"Oh, god! Cam!"

He clasped that bud between his knuckles and matched the rhythm in opposition to his thrusts. I clawed at his arms, clawed at the bed as he levered us together, apart, together, apart. Then the drilling fire began to creep up my torso.

I screamed.

Arched at an impossible angle.

"God, Kaitlin! God!"

Exploded.

Cam spasmed inside me, over me. Pulling my hair free, I reached for him and pulled him to me, savored every last tremor.

◆

When our bodies had finally settled, Cam lifted up on one elbow. With the lightest touch, his fingers trailed through my hair. I started to drift.

"That makes the second time. I thought it was the men who were supposed to fall unconscious after sex."

I blinked myself back into focus.

"Sorry."

"Don't be. Dmitri isn't the only one who's noticed how pale you're getting. You must be exhausted."

I smiled, reached up to trace the bones of his cheek.

"Just having a hard time sleeping lately. That's all."

"I noticed you are a pretty restless sleeper." His hand shifted to my face, cupped my cheek. He watched my eyes so very carefully. "Are you alright, Kaitlin? Is there anything I can do?"

Suddenly, I felt so vulnerable, so exposed, naked there beneath him. I tried to turn my eyes away. He caught me, drew me back.

"Don't, Kaitlin. What is it?"

"I just...When I was a kid, I did some..." God! The pain in my chest tried to rip through the bone of my rib cage. "I, um, made some mistakes. They just...kind of sneak up on me sometimes." I gasped as the pain snaked up my throat, strangling me. Again, I tried to turn my head away. Again, he wouldn't let me. I shivered in the cold, felt hot tears drain down the back of my throat.

Cam tried to catch my gaze. I tried to let him. But I just couldn't hold it. His hands, his intentions held me, soft and strong.

"What kind of mistakes, Kaitlin?"

"I can't..."

I couldn't think, I couldn't breathe. I scrambled out from under him, away from that penetrating kindness. After a little resistance, he let me go. I stopped at the edge of the bed, buried my face in my hands.

"I'm sorry. This is so stupid. I'm sorry."

Behind me I felt the bed move. Cam draped a soft blanket around my shoulders. He perched beside me and put his arm around me.

"Hey."

"Sorry. Hormones, maybe, I think. I'm a little out of practice."

"Four years? I'd say that's a lot out of practice. How'd someone like you manage to go four years without sex?"

I laughed as I scrubbed away the tears.

"What's that supposed to mean?"

He tucked a lock of hair behind my ear, caught the corner of my gaze.

"Well, you are beautiful, funny, and in a profession way overpopulated with testosterone. So, I ask again: how'd you make it four years without sex?"

I pulled the blanket tighter and cocked my head. "I...I guess." This time I laughed for real. "I'm not really sure. I guess the first couple years I just didn't want anything to do with it. And then when that started to fade, who did I have? I travel all the time. There was no way I was sleeping with Jessie or Gerard. Other than one-nighters, that didn't leave me too many options. Even once I remembered I had a libido..." I trailed off with a shrug.

"Oh, Kaitlin, you have libido to spare, believe me."

I arched my eyebrow suggestively at him. He chuckled and pulled me in tighter. I slid a hand out to his bare knee, traced the shape of the bones there. He was going to let it slide. But eventually he would get it out of me. I didn't need an oracle moment to figure that out. What the hell was I going to do?

Finally, I sighed.

"I still better see to your honor. Don't need Dmitri asking you for a play-by-play on the way to work tomorrow."

I felt his face spread into a grin against the top of my head.

"Dmitri's too much of gentleman."

"True, but I suspect he's in the minority."

I sat up, slid the blanket away, and rose. His hands smoothed over my sides as I stood.

"If you insist, then I will walk you back."

"I think I can find my way."

"Actually, Gerard said you'd lose your way on a straight line, if I've got the quote right."

"Can't trust that bastard with any of my secrets. First Jessie, then Gerard. When did you three get so tight?"

He raised a fist in mock toast. "Beer maketh best mates."

I shook my head with a wry grin and together we began to gather our scattered clothes.

16

He kissed me goodnight at my door.

It was soft and sweet and almost enough to have me grabbing the front of his shirt and pulling him inside. Almost.

My hand did reach out to brush down his chest one last time. He caught my fingers and gave my hand a squeeze.

"Goodnight, Kaitlin."

I gazed up into those sweet, shock-blue eyes one last time.

"Goodnight."

Then he turned to walk away and like a good girl I closed the door between us.

"Oh, god." I pressed a hand over my mouth, but I couldn't suppress the giggles. "I just had grown-up sex!" Why was that so hysterically funny? I finally had my head to myself and I was using the opportunity to lose my mind!

But I was still grinning like an idiot as I stripped away my tattered outfit and headed for the shower. The soap and hot water brought to life a cacophony of stings and aches that I'd missed over the past four years. I didn't care. I cared that he thought I was beautiful and funny. I cared that he'd rubbed my back and whispered to me in his sleep.

I tossed back the shower curtain and pulled on a towel. I flipped my head upside down and used a second towel to rub as much of the water out of my hair as I could. I would never get any sleep if I soaked my pillow. I probably wouldn't get any sleep anyway, feeling like this, but—

"You always fuck the guy who's trying to fucking put you in jail?"

I screamed, jerked upright.

Stephan stepped into the room, grabbed the front of my towel, and shook me.

"You know that's what he's doing, right? Are you some kind of goddamn blind moron?" His speech slurred as he shouted in my face; the fumes from the alcohol choked a cough out of me. His next shake brought the towel halfway down my breasts. "He's got reports!"

Even in his drunken confusion, I could feel him fingering the edges of my mind. Ashley swept in to shut me down, but she was too slow. My fury exploded.

"Keep out of my head!" I tried to yank back at my towel. I had no leverage on the slick tile.

Stephan tightened his grip, pulled me closer.

"He's got reports. That's why our fucking insider fucking blew us off."

"If he's got reports, then you're blown. Get off the ship. Get out—"

"He's got reports on *you*, Ashley!"

I knew he could feel my anger recede. He rushed into the void.

"We'll pull this off one way or another, Ash. No one checks those cans once they're sealed. People are lining up begging to give us money. Millions each. We'll pull it off—"

No one checks those cans once they're sealed.

My eyes went wide.

"You are stealing people," I breathed. Mak was the one who brought him the scam. Mak who was always in and out of jail. They weren't just going to steal people. They were going to steal convicted felons. The ultimate jailbreak.

I gripped Stephan's hand.

"You have no idea what you're doing. You could end up murdering hundreds of people. If you break the seal on that canister...if you try resuscitate someone without..."

Stephan twined his fingers with mine. I ignored it. I had to make him understand.

"Stephan, this is nothing like cracking a safe."

"It's exactly like cracking a safe. We will pull this off." He stroked at my fingers with one hand, all the while his other hand had my towel in a vise grip between my breasts. "I want you on our side, Ash. You've been gone long enough. It's time to come back. But you've got to stay away from Glaswell. He'll take you down with or without the free fuck."

I yanked my fingers free of his. He used my distraction to make a drunken lunge for me. Except unlike any other drunk, he lunged for my mind.

I ducked—as though that would somehow save me.

Deep inside me, Ashley shivered with the sensual familiarity of our joining. I shook in disgust at her reaction, with the effort of maintaining my own self in the midst of his invasion. As he stroked and lulled, I gritted my teeth.

"I will not help you do this. Get out of my head and get your goddamn hands off me."

Just like that, he did.

Just like that my toes pressing against the tiles had nothing to resist. My feet went out, my body went back, and the side of my head met the edge of the counter on the way down.

I missed a few seconds.

I must have, because when I looked up I saw the fragile young boy he had been, his face white, his mouth open in horror, his intention reaching for me. And I knew the lonely young girl was looking back at him.

"Ashley, oh, god."

Carefully, he crouched down in front of me. He gathered up one of the fallen towels. He looked at my nakedness, but right now his heart and mind were elsewhere. I got a full flash of his sister, an actual visual memory, as he gently laid the towel over me. I kept my mind still, blank. I was afraid I might shatter this new connection and something, somehow told me that this was a story I needed to know.

That tiny, pretty little girl had such a beautiful smile. *A smile like her mother's.* But as I watched, she cowered, a huge boot tossing her frail body into the air. And down the stairs. Where she lay sprawled, still as I lay now.

I promised I'd always protect you.

I promised.

My head lifted. I felt his long, slender fingers under my skull. While I'd been taking my first real trip into Stephan's mind, something hot and sticky had weighted my right eye lid shut. And my head had begun to throb wickedly.

I let out a cautious breath as he helped me sit up.

Then caught it back again as the blood rushed to my head.

I raised a shaky hand to my forehead, but Stephan gently caught my fingers before I could make contact. With a muffled groan, I squeezed my eyes shut. Stephan scooted closer to support my back. I let him.

"I'm sorry. I would never, ever—"

"I know." I turned my hand over in his, gave it a squeeze. "I know."

For a minute I just floated in the pain and exhaustion, trying to breathe through it, not succeeding. Stephan shifted behind me, brought me back.

"I'm going to help you up."

I reached up for the counter edge with my free hand; Stephan shifted his hands under my arms. Together we got me to my feet. I leaned heavily against the counter, looked up into the mirror.

"Oh, jeezus."

Her. Blood down the side of her face. Screaming and screaming and screaming and screaming.

"Whoa. You're okay." Stephan grabbed my arms to keep me from sliding. "You know what? You know what? Her name was Jemma Weir. She went on to break into many, many more houses. Except she was a fucking idiot. I'm pretty sure she's serving a life sentence right now for getting caught so fucking many times. I'll bet you could look her up. Okay?" As he talked, Stephan tried to wrap the towel around my back.

With a low chuckle, I took the towel from him and secured it around me.

"Okay," I whispered.

We shared a sad smile in the mirror.

"You want me to try to clean that?"

"I think I'll just get back in the shower."

"Are you sure?"

"Yeah."

"I'll go get you some clothes."

"Thanks."

Even though Stephan paced outside the bathroom door, his mind hovered inside with me, watching for any sign of unsteadiness. I made the shower quick for both our sakes.

I went out into the bedroom area dressed in a cotton tank top and shorts with a tissue pressed to my forehead. Stephan perched on the edge of the bed. I couldn't feel the alcohol in him anymore. I sat down next to him and we both stared at the bathroom door.

"How bad is it?" he asked.

"The cut is pretty small. I must have hit it just right. But I'm going to have a killer goose egg tomorrow."

He smiled, pulled my hair back to look for himself, nodded.

"Probably more water than blood."

I nodded back, and we slipped back into silence.

"Your sister..."

Stephan looked up in surprise. "You...?"

"I saw her when you remembered."

"How could you? You've gotten so much stronger, but you could never see before."

"She...."

"He killed her. Just like he killed my mom. Just like he'd kill me if he could find me. Sometimes...sometimes I wondered if he'd gotten you, too."

"He's dead. Presumed dead. Firefight with the coast guard."

Stephan let out a disbelieving breath. I watched as his intention rose from him and walked away. Just completely detached from him and walked dead-eyed out the door. My heart stopped for a second and I gripped his arm.

"Stephan?"

His eyes remained vacant as he stood. Alarmed, I stood with him.

"Stephan!"

He gripped my arms, but he still didn't see me.

"Ashley, come with me. One last gig. After this, we could go anywhere, do anything." The longer he talked, the clearer his eyes became. "I've loved you from the first minute I met you. When you left, I tried to understand, but it hurt so fucking bad. I looked for you everywhere." His intention slowly drifted back to him, between us now it reached for me—my face, my hair. He was making no attempt to control or conceal it. "I never stopped looking for you. And then when Mak said he'd found you...."

My heart broke hearing his words. Despite my best intentions, I had to reach a little for Jessie's Kaitlin as I shook my head.

"I can't do this with you, Stephan. I won't. And you have Amilee now. You have no business betraying her like this. She loves you."

"She knows. She knew before we came here."

"That doesn't make it right. And it doesn't change anything. I will not help you do this."

"We'll do it with or without you. We're in too far now."

"Then do what you have to do. Just know that I will do the same."

"Ash."

He pulled me to him, crushed me to him. With a hand in my hair, he pulled my head back and kissed me. I felt his tear wet my cheek. I didn't respond. Once he'd had his fill, he lifted his head, brushed the hair back from my damaged temple. Those dark, liquid eyes shimmered in the low light. When I stepped back, he let me.

"Goodbye, Stephan."

There was a hard, pained twist in his smile as he stepped past me. He pulled open the door, hesitated. When he looked back at me, that wicked, cocky glint had returned to his eye. My heart stuttered just a little.

He laughed and closed the door behind him.

◆

At 2:52 a.m., I rose and dressed for work.

The long-awaited tour was today. I chose a charcoal-gray pants suit with a satin and lace camisole that matched my eyes, dressed it up a little with a silver-gray scarf knotted at the side of my neck. I searched the closet, then realized that Stephan had claimed my other white sandal in our first skirmish. I settled for the black pumps.

Between Stephan and Cam I was going to need to go shopping.

I spent time on my hair and makeup. So far, the goose egg wasn't living up to my predictions, but I didn't feel the need to advertise my little mishap either.

I studied my artistry in the mirror.

The eyes.

I had dressed my body, but I couldn't seem to dress my mind. No matter how I twisted and stretched, after these last few days Kaitlin just didn't seem to fit anymore. Her Teflon ego and ability to skim over the surface of anything emotionally challenging...I was losing my grasp of her. I was drowning in emotional reality.

And Ashley? Her unreality jarred against the open-hearted innocence of the girl she had been. Even the battered soul that had fled Seattle that autumn night so long ago had more courage, more determination than the terrified and shattered remnant of her I hid shamefully in the recesses of my mind.

How the hell could I do my job, live my life with no defenses against the deluge?

I turned away from the mirror.

I couldn't answer that question.

I pulled my bag from the floor next to the door and dropped it on the bed. Immediately, I knew Stephan had been through it. Just little signs. My tank top was folded lengthwise, then cross; my perfume had swapped places with my lip gloss. I dug through the workout section, found my stick of deodorant. I gave the base a little twist. It didn't move. I smiled grimly.

"Take that you cocky bastard."

So,, Stephan hadn't gotten the stick with the ship's schematics on it. Mak knew I had it. Mak would come for it.

I slipped the stick back in the bag, finished packing, and slipped out of the room.

◆

I knew where most of the ship's cameras hid now. No punch-happy guards would sneak up on me this time.

This observation deck—more like a lounge—bore the title, *Breaking Free*, in beautiful gold script across the upper window. Instead of reproductions of ancient paintings or artful images of worn artifacts, this deck hosted video displays along its walls.

One holographic video showed a man in a shiny space suit and a claustrophobia-inducing helmet making his dramatic walk toward a cramped little capsule.

One showed a handsome, clean-cut man taking the podium before a crowd of media sporting enormous cameras.

One grainy image showed a kid squatting in the sand watching rocket fire disappear into the clouds.

The men from the Apollo program, the men who had strapped rockets to their chairs and gotten away with it.

Keeping to the left of the deck's camera, I slipped between two of the displays. I settled down on the thick pile carpeting, pulled my legs and bag out of view, rested my head against the display stand.

The wall of the stand rumbled against my head. I didn't look up. But I listened.

"Somewhere along the line I made a rational, coldhearted decision that, on the one hand, there was a one-in-three chance of not making it back. And I wasn't just worried about me; I thought about my family. We had no insurance; you couldn't get insurance. And we had five kids, and how irresponsible that would be.... It certainly was a negative on that side of the balance. Not to mention my own hide. Versus the other things, which were...adventure, exploration, national prestige, personal honor, and excitement... And I had decided that that was acceptable."

I closed my eyes. Just like that, huh? No comets, plagues, signs from God? Just bye honey, bye kids, see ya on the other side! For...

I opened my eyes and looked up. The projection on the ceiling rumbled me through the visuals of lift off. The blue of the sky growing thinner and thinner until finally it was no more. We continued into the pin-pricked blackness up and up. And then we started to spin. And there was the Earth, an aquamarine opal glowing against black velvet. So impossibly beautiful, growing smaller and smaller.

"Sure, it's breathtaking to look out and see the Earth. And probably if somebody'd said before the flight, Are you going to get carried away by the Earth view? I'd have said, Nah. That sort of stuff—Are you going to get carried away looking at the Earth from the moon? I would say, No, no way. But yet when I first looked back at the Earth, standing on the surface of the moon, I cried. And if everybody had ever told me I was going to do that I'd have said, 'No, you're out of your mind.' ...Whether it was relief, or whether it was the beauty of the Earth, the majesty of the moment—I don't know, just every—you know, I never would've said I was going to do that. But I did."

We kept spinning and there it was, that too-big moon in all her majesty and secret power, a chunk of hammered silver gleaming on that same depthless velvet.

The wall vibrated with the appearance of the new scene.

"I've always believed in exploration... Exploration is the greatest adventure. And exploration is why we're no longer huddled up in caves. Or no longer huddled up on the eastern seaboard, in thirteen colonies. Or why we carved this tremendous nation out of a wilderness... This spirit that took us to the moon is the same spirit that moved our forefathers west across the country. And as they carried the flag west, why, we carried it to the moon."

Risking safety, security, risking love and life. For....

For freedom, for the chance to become something more, for the chance to become a part of something greater. Insanity, maybe. I held a secret little smile to myself. But then it took a little divorce from reality to do anything worth doing—chasing a dream, loving a relative stranger, building a new life.

Okay, sometimes a big divorce from reality.

I looked down from the ceiling to the brushed steel and black leather of the seating area. I pressed my fingertips over my still bruised lips. When I closed my eyes, I could feel Cam's arms around me, the scent of him fresh and clean and salty like the sea. If we were any other two people, the physical and the mental rapport we shared would have led us easily into love. Right now, we teetered on the edge of it. And I didn't have long before we fell either one way or the other. I sighed.

I knew what Stephan's parting laughter meant. He thought he'd found a weakness, a chink in my armor he meant to exploit. A wriggling thread of fear slid down my throat and spooled in the pit of my stomach, coiling and coiling and coiling. Out of time. I was running out of time.

I looked up at the ceiling. We rocketed past planets now, past solar systems and star clusters and nebula. Finally, we began to slow. What was once invisible now unfurled in our vision: a planet marbled with greens and blues and browns, a swirling lace of clouds. Earth-like, but not Earth. Someplace...worth the risk.

"I have learned to use the word impossible with the greatest caution."

There had to be a way to take these jackasses down. There was no way I was going to let them hurt me or the people I loved. There was no way I was going to let them murder people simply for the thrill of the heist.

I'd told Stephan I'd do what I had to do. If in the end it ended up ripping the beating heart right out of my chest, then that's just what had to be.

17

A shriek from my mini woke me. I fished it from my bag and killed it. Forgotten I'd left it on.

With a silent groan I straightened. My neck hurt in a sharp, spinal sort of way that said I was going to have a killer headache later today.

Coffee.

Dodging the camera, I left the rocket men to their remembrances.

The elevator took me down to the food court. I got a little shot of adrenaline when I stepped into the seating area. The nausea and fog of sleep deprivation should have made it easy to ignore. It should have dissipated as I stood in line for caffeine. It didn't.

I looked around.

He was here, somewhere just at my periphery, getting closer.

I stepped up to the counter. A giant cup of scalding hot coffee could be an excellent weapon. But just in case I ended up drinking it....

"Grande nonfat hazelnut latte."

I moved down the counter, thanked the barista as she slid the cup into my waiting hand. Carefully, I loosened the lid.

Coming in from my right.

I turned. I couldn't see him in the breakfast crowd, but I could feel the impatience, the scorn, the disgust trying to coalesce into an action. I felt him veer away. He was going to lie in wait again.

No, fucking way.

I muscled my way through the scattered throng, carefully guarding my coffee weapon from innocent victims. I caught up to him before he made it to the hall.

"I'm right here."

Sleep deprivation could make reckless anger gloriously easy.

Mak flipped around. The broom he held as a prop came up in front of him in both fists. Recognizing pathetic, helpless Ashley, he lowered it.

"You have it."

"And you don't."

I saw a group of professionals coming toward us, operations personnel by their purple badges. Mak took a step toward me, his anger buffeting me like volcanic wind. Stephan had to be somewhere near because I saw the faintest outline of Mak's intention spark to life, his knife hand sweeping toward me. Forgetting the coffee, I took a step back.

Fortunately, that put me right in the path of the technicians. Quickly, I snapped the lid on my latte before I could damage the wrong people.

"Stay the hell away from me," I yelled.

The look on Mak's face darkened murderously. He knew exactly what I was doing and right now there was nothing he could do to stop me.

I fell in with the technicians, clipping my own purple badge on the lapel of my suit.

Amidst alarmed stares, Mak fell back, conceding the field.

It wouldn't last.

◆

Paula and Jessie looked back at me as I slipped into the office. After Paula's confession yesterday, I almost slipped back out again. The air had a definite charge to it and the way they discreetly stepped apart didn't help.

Paula smiled softly at me.

"Come on in, Kaitlin."

My return smile was strained as I closed the door behind me. I couldn't help but feel a quick spike of jealousy, which was ridiculous because it had been my idea in the first place. It gave me desperate thoughts of going back to bed until I could wake up as myself again—whoever in the hell that was.

I dropped my bag by the door and forced myself to join their little coffee klatch.

"J.C. has moved our tour up to 9:30. Cam will be joining us. I know six months is a ways off, but have you had a chance to draw up our bid for that casino project that starts at the end of December?"

I looked blankly at Jessie. He tried prompting me.

"The Shahrazad? In Vegas?"

"I saw you working on it before we left," Paula offered.

I turned my blank stare toward her.

I watched as Jessie pulled my coffee from my hand.

"Let's step outside."

The room swayed a little as I lead the way back toward the door. If my first wind had run out, shouldn't my second wind be kicking in soon? And if it did, would it last through 9:30? Maybe I could curl up under the table and take a nap. Would that be unprofessional?

We reached the hall and Jessie turned me to face him.

"Did something happen with Cam last night?"

Beer maketh best mates.

"You're keeping track of my sex life?!"

"You said sex, not me."

Gerard settled in against the glaring white wall and took a drag from his coffee. "Who said sex? Are we having girl talk? Pretend I'm not here. Tell him everything."

"Fuck off, Gerard," I snarled.

Gerard grinned as he pushed off the wall. "Promises, promises."

"Threats, Gerard. They're threats."

"Ya look like shit, Osgood. Let's all quit pretending I don't know what's going on here. What happened?"

Sure, fine. Whatever Jessie had or hadn't told him, Gerard was startlingly smart. He would have pieced most of this together. I turned to include him in the conversation.

"They have—had—an insider. The insider got scared off by some report Cam got."

"And you got this information how?"

I stared at Gerard, waiting for him to answer his own question. Unlike him, I didn't rat my friends out.

Finally, Gerard raised an eyebrow. "You're kidding."

I did a quick perimeter check with my brain, then gave it to him straight.

"He cracks safes for a living. Did you really think a sawed-off chair and a curtain rod were going to keep him out?"

"You used to date a safe-cracker? You might just be interesting after all, Osgood."

Jessie held a hand up between us. We shut up. He held one finger in front of Gerard's face.

"We will talk later."

Gerard rolled his eyes.

Jessie turned his drill sergeant gaze to me.

"The fingerprint didn't get anything?"

"No, he has switched identities with some totally harmless farmboy. Must have cost him a fortune. It's a really close match, really professional job."

"Then we get the insider to turn on them. It's a much cleaner solution."

I bit at my lip. Cleaner solution. How many weeks would it take to pick out the turncoat and then turn him on the others? One, two? Three, four?

Jessie reached up and lifted the side of my neatly pinned hair. I looked away. My little goose egg throbbed with the attention I'd so carefully withheld. Jessie's desire to reach out and shake me warred with his equally strong need to pull me in, hold me tight, keep me safe. He did neither.

"You will not be in that room tonight. Not a word. Now both of you get in there and get to work."

I turned and obeyed, but all I could think was...

Not enough time. Not enough time.

◆

While Gerard took his turn reviewing the schematics, Paula and I attempted to turn a junk heap into an office. In our zeal to assemble our tools, the boxes, containers, and packing materials had taken over the small space. We sorted and flattened and stacked up the recyclables, set aside permanent containers to be stored. I still felt pukey but moving around made it easier to ignore. I didn't know what I was going to do when it came time for the tour.

"I need to pop down to the ladies room," Paula said as she dropped the last box on the pile.

"Alright, I'll call and make an appointment with facilities to get this all carted away."

I removed my mini from its energy bar wrapper in my bag—one day I really was going to throw that away—and started tracking down who was in charge of what on this half of the ship. So much more complicated over here. On the other side, you said, *Hey, get rid of this.* And someone came and took it away. On this side, even garbage was bureaucratic.

I stood listening as each progressive person passed me on to the next even greater denial of responsibility. I wandered over to the upended container where Gerard had arranged his precious power drill. I lifted the flathead bit and played it between my fingers. Men and their tools. Stephan had had his own over-coddled array of gadgets: screwdrivers, pliers, drills, little wads of stuff that went boom.

Drills and screwdrivers.

"No, they don't fit down the recycling chute and actually we'd be happy to haul them down ourselves if you can just get someone to let us in."

"If you can bring them yourselves, I'll just prop the door open now," the woman replied.

I set down the flathead, trailed my fingers across the selection of miniature weapons.

"Okay, and where am I going?"

"The canister loading facility."

The canister loading facility.

I swept my open hand across the implements. When my hand returned to my jacket pocket, the Phillips, the flathead, and the sharpest drill bit were missing from Gerard's beloved tool set.

I smiled grimly to myself. *No, Stephan, I haven't forgotten everything you taught me.*

"Alright, I'll be right down."

18

I wasn't prepared for the punch of seeing him again.

Neither was he.

Cam's intention swept over me, seized me, the second he stepped into the room. I flushed with it. I turned to face him. The crisp white business shirt, unbuttoned with rolled up sleeves, emphasized his athletic tan, emphasized the sense that he'd just stepped away from some flurry of activity that he would soon be returning to. That shock-blue gaze locked on mine. His intention stilled, slowed, became more deeply intimate.

And then the tangle began to twist...out from him and into me.

A painful, horrible drilling into my chest.

My eyes began to tear. I looked away.

I saw Paula watching as she switched off her equipment and I gave her a weak smile. She looked over my shoulder. The drilling dulled. But the tangle remained, writhing over my skin like a mass of invisible snakes.

Paula gave my arm a quick squeeze as she passed. The concern and the caring caught me by surprise. But I savored it to ease the ache in my heart.

Maybe men had beer and women had powder rooms.

I picked up my own workpad from next to Paula's cameras. He touched me.

"You alright?"

Suddenly, Kaitlin fit brilliantly. I blinked fast, then turned with a smile plastered from ear to ear.

"Great! Is this everybody?" I felt a bitter snarl walk in the room. "Oh, Davina's joining us. Good, maybe she can introduce us to some of her people." *So, they can hate us, too. That should be fun.*

Cam's look became watchful. "How did you know she was here? You got eyes in the back of your head?"

Fuck! Fuck, fuck, fuck, fuck! I *never* did that. *Ever.*

Kaitlin pulled out a grin. "Can't everyone feel when that much joy walks into a room?"

Kaitlin marched right past the Director of Port Security and made a straight line to poor J.C. where he was absorbed once more in the disaster of the moment on his workpad. She gave his shoulder a squeeze to bring him back to Earth.

"Shall we?"

J.C.'s head snapped up. It gave him a start to see all eyes focused on him, but he quickly gathered himself.

"Yes, let's make this quick."

That tangle moved over my skin; those eyes drilled into my back.

Yes, let's.

◆

There was nothing quick about a tour of a ship with twenty decks.

Even Jessie with his unbelievable stores of self-discipline had a glazed look in his eye by the time we reached deck ten. And lord, my feet hurt! But we all had our workpads out. Most of my notes related to staff we'd met so far. I'd add it to Paula's interview prep notes when we got started tomorrow. Which reminded me, as much I'd rather not, I had some things I needed to ask Davina now that no staffers were around.

I made my way through the little group to walk next to her. She glanced toward me.

Oh, feel the love.

"Ms. Soto, we'll be ready to start compiling files for the interviews by tomorrow. Who do I contact in your organization to get access to the employee files?"

"Do you even have clearance for that? That's private information, some of it is even classified. I haven't seen any kind of—"

"Davina, they all have clearance. You were there in the meeting with Will, Arlen, and I when we discussed this." Cam turned to me and put out his hand. "You have your badge?"

I pulled my badge from the pocket where I'd stashed it after my escape from Mak. I dropped it into his waiting hand, careful not to let my skin touch his. Cam took my card, nudged J.C. to the side, and swiped it through the card reader at the door. Three green lights.

Cam returned to us.

"Full access to all parts of the ship, Davina. Full access to all ship's data, including personnel records." She looked away and I was surprised the whole hall didn't spontaneously combust. Jessie, Gerard, Paula, and I all held very still. This didn't bode well. Cam was going to have a problem on his hands.

I jolted with surprise when Cam grabbed my lapel. The back of his hand brushed my breast; his fingertips pressed into the skin above my camisole. My stomach clenched. I looked up and caught his gaze for a split second. A different kind of heat. The kind that made my throat too tight.

Would you make up your fucking mind!

He released me. I looked down and my badge dangled crookedly from the lapel of my suit.

I followed the others into the room, staying near Davina. I knew most of her anger was directed at Cam. But I still had to work with her. And primarily with her specifically as the employee records were under her jurisdiction. Arlen dealt more with guest issues on his side of the boat. Summoning my best Kaitlin, I steered her away from the main group.

"I know you are unhappy with this arrangement. Is there something I can do to make this easier for you? It's certainly not our intention to make your work environment uncomfortable."

Oh, could I ever feel how much she wanted to slap me in the face at that exact second. But she hadn't become head of Operations Security through pure chance. She took a deep breath. The tang of artificial calm filled the air. She turned to me.

"Ms. Osgood, my staff will be happy to assist you in any way you need. I report in at 7:00 a.m. and punch out at 10:00 p.m. Anyone on my staff can locate me, if there is anything you need that they don't have access to." She closed the statement with a deafening, *Are you happy?*

"Thank you." I shot her a grim smile. As I turned to catch up with the group, I gave her arm a quick rub. "Hang in there."

Her confusion pinged at my back as I walked away, but finally she settled and her constant state of rage cooled a bit. Only a few degrees, but it was still a relief.

I drew up beside Jessie as we walked through a narrow warehouse row.

J.C. waved his arm around ahead of us.

"This is where all the materials for packing the canisters are stored. If this was a regular canister, this shelving would rotate as the technicians stripped them clean of the essentials the colonists will require once they reach their designated planet."

The canister loading facility.

Behind J.C. we emerged onto a platform facing an enormous metal, well...can. It dangled on a rail from the story above and tugged at a tether on the rail a story below. A large loading ramp led up to the sealed door on the can's side. Wheeled bumpers lined the edge of the platform.

As a unit we moved forward to get a closer look. The simple enormity of the thing boggled the mind.

"Hey, can we get a look inside?"

Gerard jogged up the ramp, bubbling curiosity keeping his feet light on the ground. J.C. glowered at him. Gerard flipped the protective cover up from the keycode pad. Now it was J.C. who was jogging.

"Don't touch—"

Gerard took a step back.

"Dude, looks like somebody already tried."

19

I vaguely felt the jostle of Cam shoving past me. A hundred times more consuming was the blast of cold terror that sent me stumbling forward a pace.

I spun around.

Bloodless lips, pale cheeks, Davina stared back at me. Her body tilted to run—maybe that was just force of her intention—but her feet stayed rooted to the tire track-streaked tile.

"You've got to be fucking kidding me. Already? They must've panicked. They fucking mutilated this thing." Cam muttered. I heard him spin around on the grate of the loading ramp. He was looking for a camera with a clear shot of the door. He wouldn't find one. "The loader is parked...seriously?"

Yes, seriously. Parked right in front of the camera.

Beside me, Jessie glanced over my shoulder to follow my gaze back to Davina. He understood.

Cam rumbled down the ramp. He paused to look between Davina and me, then I let the poor woman go.

"Davina, this ship goes into lock down. Now."

"Yes, sir!"

She turned and fled.

"Jessie, I have a small investigative team, but I really need all the equipment and the setup your people—"

"I think the first thing we should uncrate is the trace wands, make sure we're not dealing with any explosives. We don't know for sure if they managed to get inside, but they could just as easily have planted something on the exterior of the canister. Most terrorists target the elevator, trying to detonate it just high enough to damage the platform when it falls. I assume you've got an explosives expert onboard?"

"Yes, sir."

Jessie nodded. "We've got one blast suit, if it comes to that." We were marching at a fast clip out the nearest exit. Jessie called over his shoulder. "Kaitlin, you know where all that equipment is, move out."

I hopped on one foot, pulling off one pump, then the other. Then I ran down the hall toward the stairwell. Only when she caught the door, did I realize Paula was right behind me.

"Well, this is new. I am so glad Brian isn't on board yet," she said.

Apparently, the thought of it had just occurred to her, because her anxiety burst free and flooded over me like water from a decimated dam. Shore it up. Shore it up. No reason for her to worry unduly.

"Just because someone tried to break into a canister doesn't mean they're aiming to blow up the whole ship," I reminded her.

"Trace wands and blast suits—"

"—are an excellent ass-covering strategy. What did you tell me that one time Brian wandered off at the mall? You weren't thinking about all the terrible things that could have happened to him..."

One after the other we hit the fifth narrow metal landing. Only eight more flights to go.

"...because I needed my whole mind clear and focused on finding my boy."

"There you go."

Five more to go.

"Besides, isn't it just the tiniest bit exciting, the thought of catching an actual bad guy versus picking up somebody who's just thinking about it, planning for it?"

Paula's laugh was breathless.

"This is why he put you in charge of sales, isn't it?"

"Are you kidding? *I* put me in charge of sales. That first sales call he brought me on? Oh, lord, I think you can imagine. That was the end of that. Now, I play chatty dumb blonde," I hit the last landing, punched open the door, "and he plays calculating ruthless warlord and we actually land clients."

"The more fools they."

We jogged down the hall, wheezing like a couple of asthmatics. I unclipped my badge from where Cam had fastened it to my lapel. We came to a halt in front of our office door. And I couldn't get the damn card in the slot.

I pressed the heel of my hand to my mouth to suppress a giggle.

"Oh, jeezus, coffee, adrenaline, and ten flights of stairs. Okay, one more time."

"Not sure I trust you with a box knife at this point."

I had to use both hands, but I got it in there. We burst into the room.

"Jessie, Box 10."

We surveyed the remaining wall of boxes, things we hadn't planned to unpack for another two months, possibly three. No point in training people on equipment if they weren't going to be around to use it.

"Box 10. Of course."

Paula pointed to a wide hardcase, four boxes down in the center of the wall. I groaned in deference to my already wobbling muscles. Each of us took one end of the conference table and hauled it out of the way. Then we got to work saving the world.

◆

Paula and I had a giant box of monitoring equipment balanced between us.

"Left. Left. Keep going. Fingers. Fingers! Up higher!"

I heard the door open.

"Whoa!"

I heard the thump of boots and Paula's end of the box shot up, leaving me bearing more of the load than I could handle.

"Oh, shit."

Cam's body slammed me from behind, catching both me and the box before we went down. The scent of him, the press of him erased what little there was left of my mind. I let him guide the box the rest of the way to the table. We both carefully eased our fingers free.

Then Cam stole a nuzzle in my hair, gave my arms a quick squeeze and the tension drained like melted ice from my body. I twisted, looked up at the sweet need in his eyes. For a second, he cupped my cheek. Then it was time to step away.

"We set a couple wands to charge." I gestured toward the wall where we had set up the rack. "We were trying to dig out the portable freight scanner. Thought maybe that might be helpful. The blast suit is in that case under the table."

Jessie and Paula came around from the other side of the box.

"Cam and I have been talking," Jessie said. "We have a question for the two of you: Would you be able to conduct a modified employee screening interview specifically regarding this incident?"

I looked at Paula; she looked at me. My gut clenched. That would certainly speed things up. But on a scale I hadn't really anticipated. I blew out a breath. All to save my little secret, save my little neck from a serrated spider claw knife. I looked at Paula, really looked at tiny, beautiful, reserved little Paula and realized that if I didn't do this, her Brian would be walking onto a ship where Mak still roamed free.

"Absolutely."

Paula tilted her head ever so slightly.

"It's going to mess up the regular interviews."

"I can help with that," I promised her. I knew from her slow nod that she understood what I meant. She wouldn't be relying solely on software for those interviews. I would be mental and emotional jelly by the end of these six months, but if it meant my life and my freedom—and little Brian's safety—then I would do it.

"Today?"

Now my head was spinning.

"Today?" Paula and I both stared at Cam.

"The attempt was made sometime in the last 16 hours. They failed. The more on edge they are, the more likely it is they'll blow the interview, right?"

Never mind that they didn't know they'd just botched breaking into the canister. What they didn't know would pit them at each other's throats. This might actually work. I used my wrist to sweep the sweat from my forehead.

"Guess it's going to be another late night."

I didn't have to look at Paula to know that she wore a poorly concealed look of terror. I gave her arm a squeeze.

"I'll handle it."

I started running it like a play through my head.

"My workpad, where's my workpad?"

Jessie retrieved it from my bag, tossed it at me.

"Alright, we're going to need a room large enough to house all 2,000 people currently onboard, preferably an empty dining hall where myself and a few others can easily wander the crowd. We'll need a podium where we can make announcements.

Gerard will need time to mount a few cameras to cover the room."

"Wait! I need to make notes." Cam grabbed his pad from the other side of the table, gave me a nod when he was ready.

"Alright, cameras. We'll need a small connecting room for the actual interviews. You'll need to make arrangements to hold the people we finger separate from one another. I'll need a button camera. Where are those? Paula, Box 2.

"We'll need to pull all your staff first, Cam, and interview them, so that we can use them when we move on to the larger staff. We'll need a database we can proof against, so we know if anyone jumped ship during the round up, make sure we don't have any stolen badges, that sort of thing. Your staff can take care of that part. First department we'll want to hit after we get critical ship's crew taken care of is the banquet's kitchen staff. We're going to have to make arrangements for feeding these people. And make sure they have access to restrooms.

"We'll need to get the booth and these two monitoring stations hauled over. Am I forgetting anything?"

I saw Jessie running my vision over in his mind. He nodded slowly.

"Monitoring stations will either need to be in a separate room or partitioned off. Maybe partitioned. Don't want that interrupting the interviews. Already figured about the video cameras. Gerard went with J.C. to borrow some of theirs."

"How long does it take those wands to charge?" Cam asked.

"'Bout an hour," Jessie said.

"Then let's break for lunch. Be back in an hour."

The others headed for the door through the maze of boxes Paula and I had created. I stayed where I was.

"I'm just going to stay here, catch a nap. I'll buzz you when the wands are ready."

Cam looked at the grey industrial carpeting on the floor. He looked at me.

"My apartment is right upstairs. You can sleep there. I'll let you in."

I got a flutter in my stomach as the mere mention of his apartment brought memories of his lips and hands to vivid life across my skin. Everywhere.

Even completely alone, I wouldn't be able to sleep there for a second.

"Thanks."

◆

After the security check point, Jessie and Paula broke off and headed for the hospitality side of the ship. I followed Cam to the elevator.

He worked as we rode. Instructions to Davina, J.C., other people I didn't know. I leaned my head back against the elevator wall and closed my eyes. Davina. How cool would she try to play it? How had she gotten this angry? What was her connection to Mak and Stephan? Was her connection even to them or was it to someone/something else entirely? I would need to see if a picture of Mak would set her off. He was the only one stupid enough to show his face. The food court had a camera. I'd already checked.

"Who would have the video surveillance files for the hospitality side of the ship, Arlen or you guys?"

"Arlen has his own set up over there."

"Alright."

Cam looked up as the sunlight poured in through the open elevator door. This short hall was lined with windows that overlooked the lower decks of the ship. I glimpsed the white expanse of the elevator launch pad as Cam led me out and down the hallway to his apartment door.

His eyes and hands focused on getting us through the door, but his awareness focused solely on me. It didn't coalesce into an intended action, just pervasive, penetrating awareness.

I followed him in and he closed the door behind us.

"So, the kitchen's there."

The living room, dining room, and kitchen had an open floor plan.

"Yeah, kinda hard to miss," Kaitlin replied. A pang of guilt flashed through my chest for throwing her in his face. I didn't know how to deal with his oscillating bouts of need and rejection.

"Right." Cam stood there awkwardly for a moment, swinging his workpad from his fingertips.

"Thanks, but I can eat while I work. Right now, I just need some rest."

I stepped out of my black pumps and scooted them under the dining room chair. I pulled my scarf from my neck, tucked it in my pocket. Then I dropped my bag against the wall, so I could slip free of my suit jacket. The jacket I hung over the back of the chair, carefully smoothing the shoulders, waiting.

That's your cue, mister.

Silence.

I felt a brush against my arm, soft as the beginnings of an intention. I got a jolt of surprise when I saw his hand rise from my arm to my face as I turned around. He reached past me and set down his workpad. He'd brought us face to face, a breath away from touching.

"You okay?"

"Just exhausted." I saw my breath push into his shirt. I turned my face up to him. The difference without my heels startled me. It took me a split second to adjust to it.

And a split second after that, I was off balance again. Cam searched my face with those eyes, searched in that way that said he saw something even I didn't know was there.

"You're not just exhausted, Kaitlin."

Adjusting the truth was part of the game whether it was a con or a sales job. With him looking at me that way, I couldn't do it. I couldn't lie. I looked away. The pain in him, the sadness, it made me sick. I tried so hard to look back.

"Hey, if this is making you uncomfortable, if this isn't going to work for you..." His intentions wrenched at my chest as he simultaneously reached for me and withdrew inside himself. Quickly, I reached up, laid my palm on his cheek.

"No. I'm sorry if you got that impression."

His relief made my knees weak.

"Then what is it?"

I shook my head. He wouldn't really understand what I meant, but he would have the truth.

"You are so painfully hard for me to read. You require such terrifying naked honesty out of me. But I can't see where it's going once you have it. I can't see...I can't see what you want...what you intend...there's just this big tangle of heat and chill and confusion mixed in with a powerful desire to rip my clothes off."

He barked out a startled laugh at that.

"I can see I'm going to have to be more careful about the questions I ask. I wasn't expecting my own psychological profile in return. I guess I forgot who I was talking to."

I smiled and let my hand fall away. In the midst of his humor, his tension vanished and the warmth that always lay at the core of him unfurled, enveloping me. I eased into it, into him, raised up on my toes and brushed his lips open with my own. His hands slid up my back, pulled me in tighter. I wound my arms around his neck.

"I really do need some sleep."

His answer was to reach between us and unbuckle my slacks. A quick tug at the zipper and the weight of the belt had them slithering to the floor. As I stepped out of them, he tugged my camisole over my head.

I worked the buttons of his shirt free, letting my fingertips brush over him until I felt the muscles of his abdomen ripple. When I reached for his belt, he toed off his shoes. His pants fell away.

"How much sleep?"

"They say twenty minutes is optimal."

"You're only leaving me ten minutes to work with here."

I smiled against his lips.

"Plenty of time."

◆

I awoke pulled so tight against him. It should have been awkward, uncomfortable. Instead it felt safe. Cam inhaled deeply.

"Whatever it is you use in your hair, promise me you'll never change it. Just keep your head away from me while we're working. I don't need to embarrass myself with a hard-on in front of my people. Might ruin my image."

I laughed and abruptly he shifted his hands from my waist and shoulder to my loose breasts. And began to knead. I groaned and arched back into him. I felt him twitch against my ass. He dropped the hands.

"Whoa, remember the security crisis. Remember the security crisis. Remember the security crisis."

Laughing stupidly, we both climbed off the bed and rushed to put ourselves back together. We had five minutes to get back downstairs and back down to reality.

In the elevator, I tried to realign my brain. Davina was going to get picked out during the security staff interviews. I had to be ready for that. I had to be ready to either tie her to Mak and Stephan or to something else entirely. I had to be ready to deflect anything she threw at me. I needed more information.

I turned my head toward Cam where he scrolled through his messages.

"Why does Davina hate you?"

Cam looked up.

"You keep saying that. She's just mad."

"No, she hates you. Why?"

I had his attention now. He watched me with a puzzled expression.

"Okay, well, her brother bid for the same job. She accused me of giving you the job just because you were blonde. I showed her her brother's bid laid up against yours. His was completely amateur. He had no idea what he was doing. I said that considering he had her to coach him; there was simply no excuse for it, either. She took it as a personal slap in the face." He shrugged. "She'll get over it. Or she'll be finding a new place of employment."

"Hmm." I turned back away, needing a minute to process the information, but Cam lowered his workpad and leaned up against the back of the elevator to face me.

"So, does this have anything to do with why you were staring her down like the Wrath of God this morning in the loading facility?"

I laughed. At my own clumsy foolishness. Fortunately, Kaitlin's breezy confidence settled comfortably over me.

"Maybe. I suspect we'll know by the end of the night tonight."

"Davina?"

"I don't know yet. That's not how this works." Oh, he wasn't going to let this slide. I used the time it took for me to turn toward him to think fast. "Look, you used to be in law enforcement, right?"

He nodded.

"You remember the stories about the old lie detectors? How they could be tricked so easily? How a strong reaction to a question didn't necessarily really mean the person was guilty? Well, this isn't that unreliable, but you still have to eliminate a lot of variables before you can start making accusations."

"You didn't have her in the booth out there in the middle of the loading dock."

No, I didn't. Get your head out of your ass, Kaitlin.

"No, but I've been doing this for a lot of years."

There it came again. This time I'd been so open to him, so attuned to him, that it hurt bad enough to catch my breath. That coiling, driving mass of mistrust speared me in the chest, right through the heart, shooting pain through my entire body. I deserved it. But it didn't make it any less excruciating.

Cam's dancing eyes narrowed.

"So have I, Kaitlin. So have I."

20

By the time we got back to the office, no one would have mistaken us for a pair who'd just taken a tumble between the sheets. Wariness colored our every interaction.

As soon as we arrived, Cam and Jessie disappeared with the explosives wands. All too relieved, I welcomed the chaos of the move.

Paula, however, was frantic.

"What the hell kind of interview is this going to be? I have no background on any of these people!"

Krissi from Hospitality had bequeathed us a two-room suite. I dragged the desk away from the wall and positioned it in front of the booth.

"It won't be that kind of interview, Paula. You will just be sorting wheat from chaff. And you'll already have a pretty good idea which is which by the time I send them up here. Cam's staff will handle the actual interrogations once we're finished. We're just going to record reactions to this specific incident. Alright?"

"I'm not a spontaneous sort of person, Kaitlin. I don't like this."

"It'll be over before you know it."

I positioned the chair behind the desk and double-checked the visibility from the desk to the booth. Paula started setting up her workpad and easel while I trotted over to the bedroom.

The bed had been shoved out of the way and the two monitoring stations with their stools had been set up in its stead. The monitor for the queue remained blank. I walked back out.

"The cameras still aren't syncing up. I'm going to check with Gerard."

Paula nodded, absorbed with syncing up her own system with the booth.

The banquet hall four doors down from our borrowed suite would have done a castle proud with its heavy draperies and gleaming wood floor. The mirrored paneling would make discreet signals to Paula tricky. Gerard hung from the top of a ladder, two hands in the guts of a camera.

"Nothing's coming up yet," I told him.

"Loose transmitter. Jus' sec." This soliloquy done with a screwdriver between his teeth.

The door behind me opened. Jessie burst in.

"Kaitlin, I need to talk to you."

He turned right back around again. I had to jog to catch up. He led me back to the suite.

"Paula, could you excuse us for a moment?"

Paula's eyes got really wide, but she hurried from the room without a word. As soon as the door closed behind her, Jessie turned on me.

"The wands didn't pick up any trace of explosives—of any kind."

Jessie was holding onto all of his emotions very tightly. Carefully, I nodded.

"Good."

"The job on the keypad looked more like vandalism than safecracking to me." He took a step closer. I had to tip my head back to keep my eyes on that stone blank face. One eyebrow rose. "Would you know anything about that?"

"Yes."

"You can visually ID these people?"

I nodded.

"You know they are going to try to implicate you, discredit you. Are you ready for that?"

I didn't answer. Yes, I'd known that, but it had sounded totally different in the confines of my head.

Jessie gripped my upper arms.

"I'll do what I can to protect you, but if they hit too close to home, you are going to have to come clean with Cam. Are you prepared to do that?"

A little tremor answered that question for me. Ashley, asleep so long now, ran her nails down every nerve in my body. But Ashley, whose life had been so long ago now, couldn't matter at this moment. Because there was Mak...and his knife. Because there was Stephan who didn't seem to understand the difference between stealing jewelry and stealing lives.

And Cam would hate me forever.

My gaze had sunk to Jessie's chest. I raised it back up again.

"I guess I'll have to be."

"Hey," Jessie murmured. He pulled me in tight and I hugged him back, needing his strength and his goodness. "It's going to be alright. You're not alone. We'll be right here with you."

Watching your contract, your careers, and your lives go up in flames.

Not if I can help it.

◆

Besides Cam, Davina, and Arlen, the Port's security team consisted of only ten other men and women. Cam gave them a brief and very official sounding description of the incident under investigation. Then it was my turn.

"As soon as we have got all of you in the system, we will need your help accounting for everyone aboard the ship. Each of you will report to a muster station and oversee the scanning of each passenger's mass transit card just as if this were a real muster drill. We must have an exact record of each person in attendance."

Cam stepped forward.

"This is critical. If even one person is missing, we will have to cover the entire ship until that person is located."

The group nodded. Out of thirteen people, only one single person didn't exude an attitude of serious attention and focus: Davina. Ignoring her beating fear, all the tiny little expressions and gestures of deception leakage that betrayed her, took too much of my focus. I had to get her out of here. I continued my little speech.

"Once you have accounted for everyone at your station, bring them directly here. Here, some of you will be responsible for recording the release of each person through your door. Others will be escorts either to the interview room or out of the banquet hall area. You will receive your assignments and equipment from Cam after we complete your check-in process."

I lifted my workpad and walked down to the end of the group.

"Please be aware that being selected for an interview is not an implication of guilt." I shot all those serious faces a big grin. "It just means Paula's getting lonesome in that interview room."

Behind me, Gerard and Jessie stood ready as escorts. Cam left to join them. If I didn't hurry this process along, we wouldn't be interviewing Davina, we would be carting her off to the infirmary. Stephan had said she'd backed out. Now I knew why: she didn't have the nerves for this business. The idea of committing a crime was a far different thing from committing one. I should know.

Dmitri stood at attention at the front of the line.

"He's clean as far as I can see," Paula told me through the earpiece.

I shared her opinion. He was also big, strong, and ex-military. I marked him off my checklist.

"Dmitri, could you walk with me, please?"

We crossed the room together to where Jessie stood. Dmitri began to grow uneasy. And I felt guilty, considering how much kindness he'd shown to me in the past.

I kept my voice low and stepped in tight with Jessie.

"Dmitri, once you finish your interview, I would like you to stay with my girl." I looked to Jessie. "There's going to be a problem."

Despite the flash of concern they hit me with, both men kept their faces blank and simply nodded. I returned to the group as they stepped out into the hall. Behind me, I felt Cam move to cover Jessie's door. A couple more officers, then onto the managers.

"Heather Black? Please walk with me."

I took her to Gerard, rubbed the button on my right sleeve. No interview.

Next. Oh, good, the guard with the anger management issues from the observation deck. And yes, he was realizing he recognized me.

"Frode Halvorsen?"

"Ma'am."

"You remember me?"

"Yes, ma'am."

"Are we going to have any problems working together?"

"No, ma'am."

Not so tough when he wasn't the one in power—and that wasn't a good sign, because I could feel that singe of anger even under the fear and embarrassment. But I sent him to Gerard. We could deal with personnel issues later.

I stepped over to Arlen. Next to him Davina's intention flickered into visibility. She wanted to puke. Alright, enough of this.

"Davina, could you come with me?"

She couldn't even open her mouth to talk. She just nodded. I walked her over to Cam. I tapped my button camera, warning Paula to get ready. Cam stared at me. He didn't like this. If Paula was my girl, then Davina was his. They'd worked together nearly as long. In the elevator my prediction had been odd, funny even. Now it was real with real consequences. He kept his expression light for Davina, but his schooled emotions couldn't hide a quiet background of anger, defiance.

He turned, held his elbow out for her, a silly, gallant gesture. A gesture of support. Davina put her hand through his arm. Her intention lost just enough potency to flicker out.

It occurred to me that I was getting used to these glimpses of incarnations. Either Stephan was nearby somewhere or sharing my mind with him had tripped something in my brain that had been dormant before. It felt more like the latter. I didn't know if I should be worried.

Once Cam and Davina cleared the room, I ducked my head behind my hair.

"Anyone else?"

"No. You?"

Gerard and I walked back to Arlen. Time to drop the pretense.

"We're done here. Gerard will take you all to the waiting room. Room service will be bringing sandwiches, sodas, coffee. It's going to be a long night, so take advantage of it while you can."

A long, long night. Because I couldn't falter for a second in my role as Kaitlin, or Ashley would have me putting Davina to shame.

I waited until the room was empty. I dropped my head back, swung my hair out loose. I felt through myself, shook out any remaining vestiges of my old, damaged self. Prayed she wouldn't have the chance to ambush me.

Time to go run damage control.

◆

Paula opened the door for Cam, Davina, and I. I nodded to Dmitri where he stood at attention next to Paula's desk. Cam led Davina to the booth. I led Cam to the observation room, closed the door behind him.

Davina took one look at Dmitri and realized the whole exercise had been a set up. I grabbed the garbage can and shoved it at her. She used it.

No, she didn't have the nerves for this business. How the hell had she ever gotten into security in the first place?

I slipped into the adjoining bathroom, came back with a wet cloth and a cup of water. Davina's manicured hands shook as she wiped her face and rinsed out her mouth. She looked so pale and pathetic, I wanted to have sympathy for her, but all I could feel was anger. This was the woman who had tried to destroy my life. This was the woman who still might.

I pulled a second chair to the desk, set my workpad on the table.

"Here, use this file."

I sent Paula a montage of pictures I'd collected from Arlen's surveillance cameras. Paula imported it into her interview file, then looked up.

"Please step forward and place your hands on the outlines on the panel in front of you."

Davina did so, pressing hard enough her fingertips went white.

"Please stand up straight and look at me. I am going to ask you a series of questions. I will know if you do not answer truthfully."

Paula began my little slide show on the screen in front of Davina as she worked through her control questions. The majority of the pictures were of random employees, guests on the ship. I caught a couple of brief spikes, nothing more than basic recognition.

Beside me, Paula's mood tensed as she moved into the real questioning. I leaned back into my chair and relaxed my body completely. And listened.

"Were you aware of the attempted canister break-in prior to witnessing it with the tour group this morning?"

"No."

Truth.

"Were you aware of any plans to break into or in any other way sabotage the canisters?"

"No."

Lie.

"Did you knowingly assist in boarding the ship anyone who had the intention of breaking into or in any other way sabotaging the canisters?"

"No."

Lie.

A full blow-up of Mak's face, features set in a cold rage as he watched me walk away.

I jerked, gripped the arms of the chair as Davina's fear shot out into the room like javelins of ice. Paula's software registered the same reaction and she flipped the slide show back to his portrait.

"You know this man?"

"No."

Bullshit.

I got up from my chair, circled the table. I tapped the image screen in front of Davina's face.

"This man attacked me in the food court with a knife." I lifted my hair, pulled down my scarf so she could see the still-swollen wound beneath my ear. "He demanded that I give him the ship's schematics. Do you know anything about that, Davina?"

I heard a rumble of voices from the observation room. Behind me, Paula gave a little start. Davina stared at me and slowly, finally began to understand just how much deep shit she was really in. Amazingly, she finally marshaled her fear—as if resignation somehow gave her strength.

"No."

I lifted the screen between us, so I could look her straight in the eye.

"There are children on this ship, Davina," I whispered. "There will be children in those canisters. Just how much murder are you willing to be responsible for?"

Davina pulled back. The door to the observation room opened.

"Dmitri, Gerard will assist you in getting Davina down to the brig."

No laughter danced in Cam's eyes now. He was livid.

A deafening horn sounded over the PA system. Seven short, one long: the call to muster stations. Cam had already given the captain his cue.

He didn't wait for the noise to fade but headed for the door. Before the door closed behind him, he caught it, turned back toward me. I couldn't hear him, but I knew exactly what he was saying: *We will talk.*

21

Of course, there was someone in line ahead of him.

"A knife?!" Jessie shouted at me.

I didn't flinch, just looked him dead on.

"What did you think it was? A hickey?"

"What's going on?" Paula asked quietly.

"Kaitlin's stalker is whole lot more violent than I was previously led to believe."

Paula pointed to her screen.

"And this guy is your stalker?"

I took a deep breath. *No Ashley, no Ashley, no Ashley. Come on, you have to hold onto it.*

"One of them."

Jessie folded his arms and raised an eyebrow.

"We will be looking for five men and one woman. I will signal you if I spot them. This one is going by the name of Maxwell McKinnis. I got the fingerprint off him. The rest of them, I have no idea."

Paula looked down at my workpad.

"They are starting to scan the cards."

Jessie dropped his arms.

"We need to get down and eat."

I nodded, started to lead the way to the door. Jessie walked over to me. I hesitated as he laid a hand on my shoulder.

"You did good, Kaitlin. Hang in there a couple more hours; this will all be over."

I looked up at that weathered face, needing to believe every word. Because the longer we waited, the more I felt Ashley starting to win.

◆

If there had ever been a longer twenty minutes in my life, I couldn't remember it. Ashley scrabbled frantically at every corner of my mind. She was truly inventive: I came face to face with Mak in the crowd. He slit my throat then and there. I collapsed in a pool of my own blood. Or...I never saw Stephan. He simply seized my mind from afar and walked me straight over the rail of the promenade. The fall snapped my neck, but I lived long enough to see the sharks tear my body apart chunk by chunk. Or...we sat around the table for the debrief and Cam announced that he knew his sister-in-law/ex-lover/long-lost stepsister, Davina, could never have perpetrated such a crime. But he knew who could: Ashley Porter, wanted for the 2042 shooting of Jemma Weir during a botched burglary in Seattle, Washington. The guards pulled me from my chair, hauled me to the cryogenics lab where they sealed me in a cryo-container. The stabbing cold finally shattered my screams.

Ashley's nightmares were endless and gruesome.

Eyes closed, I sat with my head laid back on the obscenely uncomfortable couch we'd shoved out of the way. I listened to Paula and Jessie talk about a picture her son had sent her from his visit to the grandparents.

"He actually got my dad out fishing again."

Jessie laughed quietly.

"Having kids around is healthy. Keeps you from calcifying. Keeps you young."

"I have such a hard time believing you never had any kids."

"Just never seemed to work out. Someday. So, you grew up in Colorado then?"

"Sort of. My dad was in the military."

"Really?"

So simple, so sweet, the melody rolling off the pair of them. Just getting to know each other, just beginning to think about the possibilities. That beautiful sensation lulled me, lulled Ashley. And I hoped for them; I hoped for them to find something beautiful to ease their loneliness.

Eventually, I heard a hand on the door handle. When I sat up, I was Kaitlin once more.

Gerard and Cam walked in.

"All stations have checked into the ballroom. It's not a comfortable fit. I suggest we make this quick."

I got to my feet, grabbed my pad.

"Have we got a list of people who didn't report in?"

"There are ten. Arlen will shoot us a list of those names."

I followed Gerard and Cam out the door and down to the banquet hall. We opened the doors and the cacophony hit me.

Voices, minds, bodies writhing with worry. God! And then it hit me. From behind.

Stephan tore his way into my brain, searching wildly. I stumbled, grabbed Gerard's arm. He looked over at me. Quickly, I dropped my hand.

Blank. I made my mind completely blank.

Get out!

And then he was gone. But not. Because then the room was full not just of panicking, nervous people, but their incarnate intentions as well.

"Osgood, what the hell's going on with you? We got work to do here."

Deep breath. *You used to walk through life like this every day when you were with Stephan. You used to think it made you like some kind of secret goddess, a seer, an oracle. It used to make you feel powerful. Pull out your inner dumb kid. You can do this.*

And forget that somewhere in that seething mass of souls lurked a man who wanted my blood on his hands. I raised my workpad, pulled up the interface of the ship's occupant database. But I couldn't keep myself from compulsively scanning that crowd.

"Where's the critical personnel? I want to get them out of here as soon as possible."

Cam watched me like my face was some sort of complex geometry puzzle he was just on the cusp of solving. It was everything I could do to pretend I couldn't see, couldn't feel his intention reach out and grab me by the chin.

"Everyone you requested is in the corner to your left with Arlen. I need to get up there and make the announcements."

Cam turned to go. I caught him by the sleeve.

"We're still missing ten people. If you have to do a sweep of the ship, can I still let them go?"

"Yeah, I'll need you to clear me a team of about sixty people or more. I'll need at least half to have operations clearance. Have Arlen help you pick them out."

His intention slid its arm around my waist, kissed me deep and hard. I flushed as Cam turned around and walked away.

I led Gerard in the opposite direction, ignoring him, trying to penetrate that crowd. But it was like trying to pick one voice out of two thousand. Despite Mak's unnatural rage, the general anxiety and impatience was too much for me to sift through.

We came to a stop in front of Arlen and I forced myself to focus on the task at hand. I couldn't help but notice that Arlen didn't find me quite so fuckable now that I'd gotten his comrade thrown in the brig. His real face still managed cheerfulness, but his intention watched me with wary eyes.

Overhead, Cam's voice brought the din down to a hush. He didn't explain anything, just told them that a large number of people had missed check-in at their muster stations, so we now had to conduct a ship-wide search. And thank you for your patience.

"We need to clear these people as quickly as possible. Then Cam wants a team of sixty or more for the sweep, half operations, half hospitality. Do you have the list of absentees yet?"

Arlen checked his pad. "Here it is. Well, we can take it down to nine: Will is in Switzerland. He must not have checked out. This Fortunato is an infant. I'll hunt down his mother. Maybe he doesn't have a card yet."

Impatient, I held out my hand. "May I see?"

Arlen spun it around for me. I scanned down the list.

Maxwell McKinnis.

Mak.

Behind. Stephan had hit me from behind.

Ah, shit.

I turned to Gerard.

"She warned them. Davina, she warned them."

◆

Our tidy, discreet plan transformed into a blatant man hunt. The search party took precedence over the critical staff and the banquet hall was converted into a movie theater with promises of food on the way.

Arlen and Cam split the search party between them. Cam walked with me and his group of forty to the waiting room we'd used for the security staff assignments.

"We can either gossip about it or you can make a formal announcement," I murmured.

"They need to know what to expect."

"That's probably best," I agreed.

As we entered the room, I fell back in the queue, leaving Cam to take the lead. He stepped up onto a chair to be heard.

I'd never have guessed that that lively face could turn so implacable and grim. I thought back to Ashley's little nightmare and my stomach clenched that much tighter.

"We will be looking for at least five men and one woman. We know that at least one man is armed with a knife. Do not engage them. If you find them, contact me directly. J.C. is getting you each earpieces..."

I stopped listening and braced myself to start wandering the crowd. The last time I'd walked a crowd with my senses so "on" I had been scrawny with ratty hair and a face younger than my years. I'd been Ashley. The face I wore now, the face Jessie and I had built, people tended to notice. And to pass through this crowd, I would pass near enough to feel the touch of each and every one of their intentions.

"... following employee pictures: Maxwell McKinnis, Amelia Dion, Steve Kan, Nathaniel Ma, Terry Rodriguez, and George Adams."

Get in there. Now.

I walked.

The fringe of the group was loosely packed. I made it past them, merely sensing their fear, watching their desire to either flee the room or to stoically withstand that fear. But by the middle I was bumping people to push past, pushing through their ghostly souls created by the power of raw emotion. Even the most decent, most focused people were going to feel something actionable in a moment like that. I kept my body rigid as the anger, affront, and attraction washed over me. Distracted intentions shoved at my shoulders, groped at my breasts and my ass, stroked my face. But as I wove through I felt nothing that felt strong enough to indicate an accomplice.

I burst free of the throng at the door of the bathroom. I rushed in and shut the door behind me. I heard voices rising outside.

"These aren't just missing passengers?"

"Are they terrorists?"

"Shouldn't you be using security personnel for this kind of thing?"

"What happened?"

"Who are these people?"

Cam called for quiet.

"The missing passengers are persons of interest in an investigation and I believe that it is best for everyone aboard this ship that these passengers be located immediately..."

I leaned over the counter and just breathed. My face was pale with the nausea. But I would get over it.

With one hand, I sent Cam the message: All clean.

I heard him hand out assignments. And that overwhelming emotional pressure in the room slowly begin to release down to...

A knock at the door.

"Are you alright in there?"

"Yeah."

The door opened.

Cam stood in the doorway, looking at me. I straightened, tried to rub the nausea out of my cheeks.

"You don't look alright."

"I'll be fine. Just worry about finding the bad guys, huh?"

Cam's intention looked toward the suite door, but Cam stepped forward, slid his hands down my arms. And I saw some flicker of something in his eyes, an idea forming in that baffling mind. I let my curiosity play over my face, but he just shook his head and pulled me into those long, strong arms, gave me a hard squeeze.

"We'll find them and lock them away good. Don't you worry about that."

I followed him out into the living room and gave him a smile as he left, stared at the door as it settled into place behind him. Amilee's sorrowful, betrayed eyes rose up in my mind.

Yes, go ahead and find the people who were once my world. Catch them and lock them away good.

Fuck.

22

I tossed my button camera, my mike, and my earpiece down on Paula's desk next to my workpad.

"All critical crew and a few of the kitchen staff are back at their stations."

Jessie, Gerard, and Paula rose from the clutter of couches and chairs in the back of the sitting room.

"So how much longer we gonna be sitting here?" Gerard asked.

I shook my head.

"No idea. An hour, maybe more. They've already found the room where they'd been hiding out. Nothing particularly interesting left behind. Just coffee cups and food wrappers. Some clothes. Dmitri down the hall is taking all the reports. I asked if he could pass them along." I gestured to my workpad. "You can follow along, if you want."

Paula started powering down her equipment. Jessie walked into the back room and switched off the interview monitor but left the ballroom monitor running. He came back in and picked up my pad.

"They're moving pretty fast." I couldn't tell if he thought that was a good thing or a bad thing. "Cam gotten anything out of Davina?"

"Not that Dmitri had heard. Kind of tough. Such a small team and they knew each other pretty well."

"Or thought they did," Paula said.

I looked over at her. "Yeah, or thought they did."

To my overwhelming relief, everyone's intentions were growing faint. Whether that was due to the calming of their emotions or just the effect of Stephan's attack fading, only time would tell. God, I hoped it was the latter or I might just end up one of those old hermit types who never went out anywhere for fear of crowds.

In the midst of my introspection, I found Paula still watching me. And I knew she was wondering just how well she knew me.

Even though I understood, it still left me a little sad. To distract myself I glanced around the room.

"The food won't be ready for about another fifteen minutes, but I saw coffee left over in the waiting room. Anybody want any?"

Jessie handed the pad to Gerard.

"Why don't you just bring the whole pot back? Got a feeling it's going to be a long night."

Paula looked up at him with tired resignation. His big hand ran up her back, rested on her shoulder with a gentle reassuring squeeze. Gerard caught me looking and we shared a knowing smile. And even his smile held happiness. The two good people in our lives had found each other. Things were going to be alright.

Gerard wandered deliberately toward the back room; I headed for the door.

◆

I eyed the remains of the snack trays. I didn't really know if the food would be up in fifteen minutes and if I was already hungry, then Jessie and Gerard would be ravenous. I grabbed the ice bucket from the bathroom started filling it with crackers and grapes and anything else that didn't look too wilted.

Then I went back into the bathroom for the coffee pot. I slipped it under the giant metal dispenser and flipped the lever. The spout started trickling before the pot was even halfway full. I groaned.

"Sorry, I stole a cup."

I spun around.

"Amilee! What are you doing here?"

I looked over her shoulder, but I couldn't see anyone in the bedroom behind her. I reached out. I didn't feel anyone nearby. Fucking distracted not to have felt her coming! Asleep on my goddamned feet.

"Oh, don't worry. It's just us girls."

I reached behind me, flicked off the coffee dispenser. "You need to get out of here."

She did her barely-touching-the-ground pixie walk around the displaced chair where Cam had stood just an hour before. She wore the staff uniform of white button shirt with a black skirt and tie, but on her the tidy outfit looked flirty. She stopped an uncertain distance from me.

"So, you're going to abandon me again?"

I eyed her guileless expression warily, but all I saw was her faded intention reaching tentatively toward me. Amilee just smiled.

"Come on, the three of us were perfect together, Ashley. We pulled off the most incredible jobs! And I need my best friend back. Who else is going to watch old Jane Austen movies with me? Not Stephan. He's great in bed, but he's not you. He simply doesn't understand the orgasmic joy of chocolate covered pretzels dipped in marshmallow crème." She laughed, so much exactly the same girl I remembered that it twisted my heart to think how I was about to betray her.

She stepped closer.

I stepped toward the door.

"Come on, Ash. You've always been my best friend. Stephan had me half-convinced you were dead. But look, here we are again, and it can be perfect. Let Mak hang. He's a wack-job anyway. Stephan has a way out of here. We'll be gone and halfway back to the islands before they can finish searching the ship."

I took another step; she mirrored me, got close enough to touch me.

"It'll be just like before, that incredible rush, the parties afterward. Hangin' out while we scope out the houses.... You're trying to get to the door." She looked so hurt, felt so hurt. My stomach turned. That whole world I'd left behind, the whole world I'd rejected had somehow become everything to her. It wasn't just her face that hadn't changed; it was her. Just like I clung to Ashley as everything weak and disgusting in me, she clung to Ashley as everything good and perfect in her life.

Oh, jeezus.

"Ami—"

"You know what those people are going to do, don't you? They are going to connect you with us and they are going to put you in jail. They don't give a shit about you."

"They do give a shit about me. But they also give a shit about right and wrong, Amilee."

"So, they'll judge you by what you did when you were young and stupid. Ash, I don't care what you've done. I'll always be there for you. You know that."

I had to break this off, end it. Her pleas were having little effect on Ashley, but I couldn't risk it, couldn't risk succumbing to some misplaced sense of loyalty.

"You need to get out of here."

I turned, but she grabbed my arm and clung.

"Come on, Ash, I'm getting you out of here. You left me. I'm not leaving you."

Now Ashley stirred.

Oh, no. Fucking forget it.

I twisted back around, faced Amilee dead on.

"I'm not the person you remember anymore, Ami. I haven't been that person since the minute I got up the courage to walk out the door and never come back. My name isn't Ashley. And it never will be again."

I shook her hand off, caught a terrible wave of pain. I didn't, couldn't look back, but went straight for the door.

Her sad, sad voice trailed from across the suite.

"The guard's not there, Ashley."

◆

Dmitri wasn't there.

I ran down the hall toward the interview room. Ami would be long gone by the time Jessie and Gerard got there, but if there was even a chance....

I threw open the door, but it hit something mid-swing. I shoved, but it didn't move. Through the crack, I could see the interview desk lying on its side.

Pain, pain, pain. Ice cold pain.

White hot pain, spreading, consuming.

"Oh, god!"

I rammed at the door. It gave; I stumbled into the room. The obstruction was Jessie.

Cold, so cold.

I dropped to my knees. My hands hovered over him, not knowing where to touch, so much blood. His chest had three holes in it, meat and bone and red, red blood. I couldn't look. I grabbed his face between my hands.

"Jess—Jessie. Oh, my god."

My thumbs stroked those wonderful crow's feet at the corners of his eyes. His eyelids fluttered, but they didn't open.

The spectre of his intention became so solid between us that I had to pull back. It raised its cold hands to my face. I closed my eyes.

"You can't go, Jessie. I can't...not without you. This is my fault. Oh, god."

I felt his lips brush mine. I thought I felt his breath brush my face. His thumb drew away my tears.

"Kaitlin."

I opened my eyes. Those beautiful hazel eyes didn't open; blood streaked his lips as he whispered.

"You're going to be strong. You're going to get these guys. Take...take care of Gerard for me."

I clutched at him, but the blood poured from his lips now. His big, strong body jerked and shuddered. His intention tried to hide my face in its shoulder, held me tight and close as it grew stronger and stronger.

"Jessie, you hold on." I tried to stand, but he wouldn't let me go. "Please, somebody help!"

"Paula...sorry."

"I'll tell her. I'll tell her. Jessie, you've got to—"

The connection snapped tangibly. Jessie's intention, Jessie's soul, rose with me still folded in his arms. He raised my face, kissed me so tenderly.

I love you.

"I love you, too. I owe you everything. I won't forget that, not for a second. Oh, god, where...wherever you're going...be happy. Please."

He smiled down at me, brushed his fingers through my hair like he'd always wanted to.

And then he was gone.

23

I knew those screaming sounds were mine. I buried my face deeper into Jessie's arm to try to block them out.

I felt Paula walk in.

"Oh, my god." There was a long pause, punctuated by curses. "Cam, Jessie's been shot. Kaitlin's covered with blood—"

"I'm five seconds away. Call the infirmary. Shit, there's nobody in there. I'll take care of it."

I heard her steps draw closer. The fine bones of her hand closed over my shoulder. I cringed. I'd taken him away from her. I'd killed him. I couldn't face her. I couldn't.

"Kaitlin, are you okay?"

"He's dead. He's dead."

"Kaitlin, I think he's still breathing."

I whipped my face around.

"He's dead! I saw him die!"

Paula jerked back in shock, but she quickly reached for me again.

"You need to calm down, Kaitlin. Are you hurt?"

I registered the subtle stirring of someone in the sleeping room. I jumped to my feet, knocking Paula back on her butt. I saw a shape solidify out of the dark. I rushed forward. Not Mak.

"Gerard!"

"Jess?"

Gerard stumbled toward the doorframe, but the blood from his chest spilling down his shirt had left his head empty. I caught him around the waist. He was too heavy. We went down. My back hit the leg of the overturned desk, the leg snapped off, and we hit the floor.

"Can't breathe," I whispered.

"Oh, shit." Paula rushed over, but Gerard was twice her body mass in dead weight.

Stephan picked that moment to invade my mind. My body jerked, he hit me so hard with his panic. He knew what had happened. He'd had to get close enough to reach me, to see if I was alright. He was going to get me out of here.

Like I'd learned to slam the door on Ashley, I slammed the door on him.

It worked.

"Kaitlin, hey." That was Cam. Cam was safe. "Let's get him off her."

The hot-cold pressure of Gerard's limp body rolled away and I drew a jagged breath. I opened my eyes and turned my unfocused gaze toward Cam. He stripped away my suit jacket, ran his hands over my torso. His fear beat down at my body like hits on a drum. The thump of it scrambled my agony into a tight curdled mass in my chest.

His feather-light touch moved to my face, hesitated over the lump on my temple, moved on.

"None of this is hers?"

"I don't think so, but I don't know."

Cam's face drew close to mine. That bright light in his blue eyes; that light that was gone forever from Jessie's. God, how could that be possible? How? How? Tears smeared the image of Cam's concern.

"Do you think you can sit up? The medics will be here in a second. I need you to tell me what happened here, Kaitlin."

I gave him a small nod. Between us, we pried me up off the floor. I winced. That table leg had given my back a brutal beating.

"All the way up?"

I pushed at the floor. He slipped his arm around me and lifted.

And then it started. I tried to hold it off. Maybe I could make it to the bathroom. Maybe no one would see.

It was too fast.

My head snapped back. My vision shifted. The room vanished, replaced by the tunnel of a jagged cave. In the distance: Mak, Stephan, and Cam ran toward me, Mak with his deadly fire, Stephan with his ice-cold control, Cam with his writhing tangle of snakes.

"What's happening, Paula? Is she having a seizure? Oh, god, look at her eyes."

"Pain, so much pain. The hunt will force your choice: Which trust will you protect? Which trust will you destroy? It will end tonight."

24

I awoke on a mat on the floor.

In front of me, the metal legs of a hospital bed rose high above me. I swept the sheet to the side. I knew by the smell of it that I was dressed in Cam's business shirt. Someone had done a cursory job of wiping the blood off me. My skin still felt tight and crusty in places, my hair crisp.

I rose on legs as insubstantial as air. I saw Gerard, his chest covered with bandages, his arm and forehead covered with sensors. The tube of an IV ran into one of the monitors. I floated over to him, touched my fingers to the gray skin of his face.

His eyelids cracked just enough to part his eyelashes.

"Osgood, see you finally spent the night. Was I good?"

Tears of relief wavered in my vision, then fell. I smiled at him.

"You were incredible."

His grin twisted toward the end.

"Shh," I murmured, stroking his cheek.

He tried to breathe through it, but it just seemed to make it worse.

"You're going to get the bastard that killed Jessie, that Mak. You're not going to go all fucking pansy-assed on me, are you?" he whispered through gritted teeth.

"I promised him."

I heard a little click and the color of Gerard's IV changed slightly. A second later, he passed out. I kept stroking his cheek.

"And I promised him I would take care of you, too, you over-sexed jackass. How I'm going to do that, I have no idea."

Cam walked up behind me, his intention reaching for me, running its hands over my shoulders and back. But underneath the want and the worry, stirred a twisting anger.

"You're awake."

I turned to him. That airy feeling spread from my legs through my torso, out through my arms and my head. I felt so small and lost under his scrutiny, before his anger. He wiped my tears away. Then he turned away.

"Come with me."

Dressed only in his buttery soft work shirt and my panties, I followed Cam through the ship and up to his apartment. Fortunately, most of the ship's occupants were still safely locked away in the ballroom.

Cam closed his apartment door behind us. The click of that lock had a horrible sound of finality to it.

Cam laid his workpad down on the small wooden dining room table, gestured for me to take a seat.

"J.C.'s people took a look at your systems. He was trying to find out if any critical data had been compromised."

I sat down on the edge of the rough linen seat. The lines across my back where the table leg had caught me thumped painfully. I clasped my hands in my lap and forced myself to concentrate past the pain and the white-hot heat of grief walling me off from the rest of reality.

"What they found was this."

He turned on a file and I found myself looking into my own eyes. Me in the ballroom, me in the interview room, me in the waiting room.

"Your software only dedicates one line of input from the subject. All other cameras focus on you, your face. It's your reactions that are being analyzed."

I turned my gaze up to him.

"What good would that do? Did you talk to Paula? That makes no sense."

"Arlen is talking to Paula right now."

I let my suspicion, my irritation show on my face.

"Then why did you drag me half-naked through the ship to talk to me about it? You know I don't know anything about how the software works."

"Don't play dumb, Kaitlin. Don't tell me you don't know about this!"

I shouted right back. "I watch her damn screen while we're doing the interviews. It doesn't show my fucking face!" I batted away fresh tears with shaking hands. "I can't take this from you right now." I pushed up from the table. "You can take your mistrust and shove it up your ass. I've had enough of your goddamn endless suspicions."

He stepped over to block my exit.

"You don't tell me. Anything. Ever."

"I told you everything. You just didn't listen."

I spun around to take the other direction around the table. He grabbed my arm.

"Kaitlin."

I stopped. But I didn't turn back around. He dropped his hand.

"I think maybe I did listen. I think I just didn't understand what I was hearing."

Slowly, warily, I turned to face him. He stepped back, gave me enough room to step out from behind the table.

"Can you trust me just for a second and not flip what I'm saying around or dodge it or redirect it back at me?"

"Could you do the same?" I asked.

Cam took a deep breath, let it out.

"Yes."

I watched him carefully. His vague incarnation slowly calmed and those penetrating, twisting attacks softened and faded.

I nodded to him.

He wandered toward the living room and I followed.

"That first time I demanded your secrets, you told me a bunch of disjointed nonsense: *Davina hates you and Will. Will is genuine. Arlen wants to fuck me.* I thought you were fucking with my head. But then I started watching you. You always knew who had just walked in the room. You could gauge my mood, despite my best poker face. You picked Davina out the second we discovered the hacked-up keypad. You always had an explanation or a brush off. And then I saw you walk through that group of volunteers in the waiting room and I thought it was going to kill you. You're not reading micro-expressions."

Confronting Paula was nothing like being confronted by Cam. I stared at him, clenched my hands on the shirt's hem to block out the trembling. I told him I'd trust him.

I shook my head, my eyes never leaving his.

"What are you doing, then?"

I opened my mouth, closed it. Jessie had never believed me.

Cam stepped closer, took my hand, and led me to the couch. We sat down, and I smoothed the shirt down over my naked thighs. Cam's intention wanted to help me with that.

I laughed.

"What?"

I looked up from my lap. My smile was pained.

"You're never going to want to be around me again."

"Try me."

"I read intentions: what you think you want to do."

I had to give him credit. He quickly schooled his disbelief.

"How?"

"If you haven't made up your mind yet, I get just a buffeting of emotion like hot wind or icicles jabbing at my skin. Not that simple, but I physically feel them. Sometimes if they are strong enough they..." I thought of his venomous doubt. "...they can punch their way inside me."

"And if I have made my mind up?"

"It depends." I looked down at the tips of the shirt tail on my lap, picked at a loose thread. "Sometimes I feel specifically what you want to do. More rarely, I can see your intentions become incarnate and begin enacting it."

"Okay, that's creepy."

"It can be. Some people's passing thoughts can be very private. I do my best to respect that. We're all human."

Cam nodded, leaned against the back of the couch.

"Who knows about this?"

I shook my head. "Jessie relied on my 'intuition' pretty heavily, but he didn't really believe me. Gerard—who knows what goes on in that mind? Paula knows."

"And Paula's your software developer?"

"I can see what you're saying, but if that were true, our software would be useless once I left the jobsite and it's not."

"It's not. But it's not as effective as it is when you are onsite. See, I already talked to Paula. She says she was under orders from Jessie to use separate software that focused on your facial expressions during onsite interviews."

He leaned forward again, stopped my fingers from their picking.

"You are the two percent, Kaitlin."

I jerked my hands away and shoved off the couch. I hugged my arms as I paced in front of the sliding glass window. Finally, I stopped in front of the darkness of the window. I pressed my face into my hands.

"That's why...."

Cam rose, came up behind me. He put his hands on my shoulders, pulled me back against him.

"That's why what?"

"He told me to tell Paula, right before he died he told me to tell Paula he was sorry. I thought he meant... I thought he meant he was sorry they didn't...," I took a deep breath, "...get more time together. Oh, jeezus."

I rubbed furiously at my eyes with my borrowed shirtsleeve. He wrapped his arms around me, rested his chin on my head.

"Think that's why they stopped letting you look at the software?"

I wrapped my hand over my mouth to keep from sobbing. I'd trusted Jessie with my soul. He knew how much it meant to me not to be associated with any kind of crime. How could he do this? How could he do this and lie to me?

But I knew. I closed my eyes against it, but I knew.

Paula had told me. That kiss goodbye had told me. He had created me to be pure and unattainable. Paula he could soil as he liked.

God.

"I would have done anything for that man. Anything."

"Kaitlin, hey." Cam turned me around, let me burrow into his shoulder. "None of this means he didn't love you. Okay? Even I know that much, alright? Even me, the plain old mortal."

I laughed into his shirt. And me, the Oracle of Delphi, I knew that, too. Somehow, someday, I would figure out how to separate that from the betrayal. Someday soon. Because I couldn't hate him. I loved him too much.

Cam pressed his cheek against my hair.

"I have more questions. No, don't tense up like that." He rubbed my back until I found a way to relax against him. "But first I'm going to feed you."

"Sacrifice your best goat?"

Cam chuckled. "Probably more like cheese and crackers."

◆

We sat at the dining table with the take from our raid: five stale crackers, a brick of cheese with the mold peeled off, fresh bananas, and a carton of yogurt only a day past its expiration. Cam popped a cracker in his mouth.

"Now this is living."

"You definitely notice flavors more at midnight," I agreed.

I bit off the last hunk of banana and let myself experience the bright tang with its underlying custardy sweetness. I folded the peel neatly on the table. Then I turned in my chair to face him.

Cam reached out and snagged another cracker.

"So, when I was talking to Paula—"

"Is she alright?" I pressed.

"Uh, yeah, she's taking everything kind of quietly."

"She's too careful with her emotions. She ends up shattering herself."

Cam nodded slowly. "I'll keep that in mind. Keep an eye on her."

"Thanks." I offered a quiet smile. "So, what did she say?"

"She said this Mak guy has been stalking you. She said you actually had more than one stalker. Were all six of them in on this? Has this been going on the entire time you've been on board?"

I gripped the sides of my chair; the banana went sour in my stomach.

Cam frowned. "This has been going on the entire time you've been on board."

I nodded.

"Can you tell me what happened?"

I would rather puke. I closed my eyes for a second. Deep breath.

"The first night they grabbed me out of the hall. They made threats, but I got away. On three separate nights the one named Stephan broke into my room. Mak approached me twice in the food court. The woman, Amilee, got to me in the waiting room a couple seconds before the shooting. She was probably distracting...um distracting me. Gerard said Mak was the shooter."

I opened my eyes, stared at my knees willing myself not to lose the banana. Cam was so angry. I wiped the sickly sweat from my face with the sleeve of his shirt.

His voice was quiet when he spoke. "Why didn't you tell anybody about any of this?"

"I told Jessie some of—" I had to stop and bite my lip, had to keep it together.

"And he didn't tell me?"

I looked up. "Why don't you just tell me what you know, so we can frickin' stop playing this game? You said you would trust me, but you're sitting there playing cat and mouse. What was in the report about me that made you so damn suspicious?"

Cam dropped back in his chair. His face was so neutral, but his emotions raged like a war between heaven and hell. Then abruptly he reined it in. The battle didn't stop, but he made his decision over the top of it.

"Alright, just that the federal government had issued you a new identity at the special request of some Senator with a really good committee seat." I raised an eyebrow. That was news to me. "And at the time, I'd just gotten a report saying there was a plot to steal prisoners out of the canisters. Rumors in the prison system. Talk about an insider."

"That's why they're here. Davina told them that I would be here with access to the schematics."

"So now you know what I know. Why didn't you tell me what was going on?"

Nope, couldn't sit still anymore. I got up and stood at the back of the couch with my back to him. My fingertips traced the cold, smooth standard issue upholstery.

"I know them."

"You know them!"

"Not all of them. I...from before. Stephan...I ran away from Stephan."

"Ran away. The name change."

I nodded. I pressed my fist against my stomach. Prayed he wouldn't ask for more. I almost wished Ashley would come back to life and take over, let me escape. Like the coward I was, I reached for her. But she was nowhere inside me anymore. I was on my own.

Cam came to stand beside me, just outside the periphery of my vision. He reached for me. I flinched, scooted further down the couch.

"Kaitlin what happened? What did he do?"

"I don't talk about it. I think it's time for me to go."

I made a break for the door. He was already there. He leaned back against the door.

"How 'bout we make a trade? I tell you the real reason it's so hard for me to let my guard down and then you do the same."

Right now, all I wanted was to make it through that door. I was done. I didn't know what he planned to do with my pathetic confessions, but he had enough as far as I was concerned. He could either destroy me or spare me. I had no control over it now.

Cam reached out, tugged at the collar of my shirt, traced the V of exposed flesh at the neckline. My blood warmed despite my queasy, cold fear. But his intention wasn't thinking sex. His intention was looking everywhere, but at me.

"You know I...I used to be married. Straight out of the academy. We'd been married a couple years and I come home after a shift. The house is empty. I'm looking everywhere. I call her, and the number is disconnected. Then I get to the kitchen. There's a pad on the table. There's a note. Says she lost the baby—I didn't even know we were expecting. Asks if I could sign the divorce papers. That's it. That was three years ago. Nobody could understand why I would go for a job like this, totally isolated in the middle of the Pacific. Well, that's the story I don't tell them."

I stared at him. He could control that matter-of-fact look on his face, but he couldn't control the wrenching pain on his other face, the ghostly tears. I reached up to where his fingers toyed with the button on my collar. I wrapped his hand in both of mine. He'd lost his baby and his love. I'd lost my innocence and my life.

Okay.

"I fell in love with the bad boy. I was just too naïve to understand he really was bad. He was into breaking and entering—home safes were his specialty. And he was into drugs and alcohol. The thing is...he was also kind of like me. He can't read other people, just me. But he can do more than read me, he can climb inside my head, manipulate me, control me. And when we're linked, he acts like an amp for what I can do. I can read people far away; I can see intentions become incarnate; I go all oracle with these crazy visions. So, he would use me as a lookout. But I hated it. I hated what I'd become. And one night he gave me a gun. That freaked me out. I got so distracted that I didn't notice this girl come in."

I had to stop for a minute. I let go of his hand to rub my face.

"I came this close to shooting her in the face. The bullet hit the wood door frame. She started screaming and there was blood everywhere. He told me the fucking thing wasn't loaded. That night I stopped wondering how the hell I was going to get out of that mess. By the end of the week I'd packed my bag, left a note for my mom, and hitched a ride out of town."

"Wow." He used his finger to raise my chin. "Wow. How the hell did you get from there to here?"

I shook my head. "I didn't. Jessie..." *Jessie.* I saw his face and my heart squeezed so tight tears wobbled again. I laughed. "I cased him for weeks. When I finally moved in on him, I worked him over good. I was so helpless and pathetic. By the time I was done, he had no choice but to ride to the rescue. He put me through rehab. I got access to a workpad, started doing research, convinced him to change his business model over to security technology. When we started landing contracts, he wanted to hire me officially. That's when he gave me the new name."

I twisted my head away. "He gave me everything. Everything. And I gave him Mak."

I lost it. I stopped even trying to hold it back. Jessie was gone. He couldn't be gone. I needed him. Every day I needed him. He couldn't fucking be gone!

Cam pulled me to him and I wrapped myself around him. And felt his tears wet my hair.

25

"You should probably get some sleep. I'm going to have somebody bring your things up here. And we'll have to do something to improve your personal security at least until these guys are caught."

I frowned into his shirt.

"Gerard already tried an oh-shit button. Stephan lifted it before I could use it."

"Then we'll come up with something more subtle."

I straightened and pulled away. I saw the dried flakes of blood left behind on his T-shirt. I gestured at the mess.

"You mind if I use your shower?"

"Come on."

He led me down the hall. Strangely his bathroom was smaller than mine. But copper tile shimmered in clever geometric patterns over the floor and lower walls, giving it a far classier look. Cam pulled me inside.

"I do believe this is mine."

I looked down as he released the first button on the shirt. Though the fabric didn't move, his intention caressed my breasts ever so gently. I bit my lip. Cam drew his finger down the newly exposed skin until he reached the next button. A little twist and it came free. He traced me down to the next button, then the next, then the next. With just a little nudge, the fabric fell from my shoulders, slid down my arms, fluttered to the floor. His intention took a little nibble of first one nipple, then the other. My center clenched. He hooked his fingers on the sides of my lace panties and pulled them from me, waited patiently until I stepped clear of them. Then he tossed them away.

He rose.

"I need to make a few calls. Get an update on the search."

"Um-hmm."

I grabbed the front of his shirt and pulled him in.

"Then you might want to tell your intentions to keep their hands to themselves."

I pulled his head down to mine and let him know with a kiss just how much havoc they'd already caused with my hormones. I felt him go hard against the softness of my stomach. By the time he drew his mouth away, he was breathing fast. He rested his forehead against mine with a groan.

"You are a wicked, wicked woman. Are you seriously going to send me out there with a hard-on?"

He glided his hands down my bare back, cupped my ass and began kneading. His intention was already sliding inside me. My head fell back as I moaned. Cam leaned in to graze my neck with his teeth.

"This...is definitely something I'm going to have to explore. But now at least I know I won't be suffering alone."

"Oh, god, and you call me wicked."

I drew my head up and he pulled his hands away. His intention stole one last caress as he slipped out the door.

"Cheating," I called after him.

I heard him laugh.

◆

I slipped into his bed naked.

And alone.

The feel of those crisp, cold metallic sheets sliding over my hot aching body brought a hum of pleasure to my lips. The room, my head, felt so blissfully empty. I no longer had that sensation of an overcrowded brain—Kaitlin and Ashley battling for control of my psyche. They weren't gone, not completely, but they had lost reality over this last week. Maybe Jessie would be disappointed that I'd never grown to fill out Kaitlin like he'd hoped. But I didn't think so. I think he'd be happy I could finally stop fighting just to be. That I'd finally settled on a me.

I rolled my head to the side, savoring the crinkle of the pillowcase, the cool press against my cheek. I stared at the empty pillow beside me. Some would say we'd just jumped straight into bed. They wouldn't realize we'd had twelve months of courtship over the phone, safe and platonic, and probably the only way either of us could have come to trust a partner again.

Either of us.

Because in my self-absorption, it had never occurred to me that he could be harboring a pain so deep.

Losing a baby.

Losing a wife.

I couldn't imagine it.

Wished he'd never had to experience it.

Because he wasn't there, I reached over and stroked the place where his head would have lain.

I heard the door open.

Him. So easy to recognize now that I knew what I was feeling: that little bit of fear hiding even now in the back of his heart.

He slipped in through a ray of moonlight. I saw the outline of my suitcases and my bag. He let them slide quietly to the floor next to the door.

"Are you awake? We're switching to shifts."

I sat up, holding those wonderful sheets to my breasts. He sat down beside me on the bed. He had a new shirt on. I worked on the buttons as he whispered.

"They found two of them, Nathaniel Ma and Terry Rodriguez."

My hands hesitated over the last button.

"Amilee said she and Stephan had a way off the boat. There's a chance..."

Cam cupped my cheek in his hand, raised my gaze.

"That we won't find them? Don't think like that."

I sat up straighter and nodded. I hadn't forgotten everything Kaitlin had taught me. But I hadn't forgotten everything Ashley, the real Ashley, had known. And this, right now, in the shadows, in the perfect moonlight, would not be about me. I pushed that last button through the hole.

Drawing my feet up under me, I let the sheets fall away. I wanted to take my time, undress him slowly. His intention brushed at my breasts. I kept my attention focused on tugging his cuffs free of his hands. I rose from the bed and drew his shirt away, laid it neatly across the nightstand. I turned back to him, savored his breath on my skin as I pulled his T-shirt free and lifted it over his head.

Beautiful.

Strong shoulders, solid chest—muscle enough to offer safety and support. Not so much to leave me feeling powerless. He was long and lean and...perfect.

I lowered myself to my knees in front of him.

I let him look his fill as I worked his laces loose, placed each shoe precisely so in front of the nightstand, set each sock carefully folded beside them. I ran my hands up his calves. I pressed my face to the inside of his knee and arched, wanting. But not yet.

I rose.

I took his hand and drew him up to standing, drew down his slacks and underwear, felt his erection spring free into my hair. I slid myself slowly up his body, letting the long silken strands caress him. Then I pushed him back onto the bed. He let himself fall.

I crawled my way up him. I planted a hand on one side of his head, used the other hand to draw my hair away so it wouldn't shadow his face. I looked into those slumberous, mysterious eyes. Just looked as his intention ran its ghostly hands over my body.

Cam raised a warm palm to my face.

"What's this?"

I let the want, the vulnerable need slide over my face, let him watch it.

"I want to love you. If you'll let me."

That fear spiked from his chest to mine. I placed my hand over it.

"Shh."

I pressed my hand down against the hurt, used my other hand, my lips, my hair, my breasts to show him peace. I stroked my way down one side, across his chest, down his torso. Our two centers met and I groaned, arching against him. His arms came around me and he rolled us over.

He rose over me, pulled my hand from his chest, and kissed my palm.

"We never did this, did we?"

He released my hand and those strong, smooth fingers stroked my face, brushed back each strand of hair. Then he slipped his hand under my head and cradled it in his palm. He held us eye to eye, that gaze I'd feared could see my very soul.

And then I felt it.

He wasn't using his body to love me, he was using his desires. Ephemeral hands moved over my stomach, ghostly lips plucked at my nipples. I tried to throw my head back, but he held me tight, drank in my soundless scream. I obeyed incorporeal commands to open my thighs to him. He held my head still, watched me as I thrashed and cried out at the torture he meted out with his mind alone as his intention spread me, explored me.

I clutched at the arm that held me fast.

"Please!"

His dark eyes looked dangerous in the shadowy light.

"I could watch you all night."

His intention rammed inside of me.

I screamed, but it wasn't enough.

"Please!"

"All night."

He reached between us and suddenly I was shot full of heat, sensation, too much, too much sensation. But still he didn't let me go.

He watched as he rolled my nipple between his thumb and forefinger. He watched as our bodies slammed together over and over and over. He watched as my breath strangled in my throat and I screamed one last time. He watched as my head lolled in his hand as he finally took us both home.

26

2:58 a.m.

I groaned silently into my hand.

I had tried so hard. But the idea that Stephan and Amilee had somehow gotten away, the idea of Mak loose somewhere on this ship, it tore at me and tore at me until I was soaked in chill sweat. I glanced over at Cam, so peaceful in sleep. And definitely used to having the bed to himself. I smiled.

I carefully slid myself from beneath his sprawled form. Lifting my bag and one of my suitcases, I slipped from the room and quietly closed the door behind me.

In the living room, I dug through the suitcase, pulled out a lace and silk nightgown that suited my idea of a nice "morning after." I drew on a pair of lace underwear that I hoped didn't clash too badly. I didn't want to risk waking him by turning on a light.

I fished my workpad and my tube of deodorant from my bag. I popped the bottom off the deodorant, let the file stick drop into my hand. Just seeing it, just feeling the insubstantial weight of it in my hand made me want to snap it in half right then and there. Jessie had died for this? This stupid piece of....

No thinking about Jessie. I didn't think my body could withstand another crying jag so soon. I popped the schematic file into my workpad, reassembled the deodorant tube, and dropped it back into my bag.

I curled up with my workpad on the couch and brought up the schematics. There were four of them left. Where could they be hiding? Stephan had a way off the ship. What could it be? My eyes were too tired to focus on blue lines. I dropped my head back on the arm of the couch.

Really, I didn't understand why they needed these schematics anyway. They knew this ship well enough to find me, no matter where I went: to the pub, to the food court, the waiting room. Didn't matter where. They always found me. The thought shot a little rush of adrenaline through me. I opened my eyes just enough to glance at the door, verify it was closed.

I could have murdered for a sleeping pill right about now.

But I knew I couldn't trust myself with the damn things.

No thinking about Jessie.

Where could they be hiding? I wasn't as smart as Stephan, not as clever and crazy, but if I were... They couldn't have their own boat. I was light on my grasp of the details, but Jessie had briefed us on the basic array of sonar and radar that a ship this size had to be equipped with, plus the satellite feeds from the space station above us. Unless I was missing something critical, they just couldn't have their own boat.

So, they were hiding, waiting.

They were still here.

Think! Think!

I slid the workpad off my lap.

I sat up.

It was three o'clock in the morning. The whole ship was asleep. Could I...could *I* find them? They had to be somewhere near where the tenders launched or the supply ships docked. They couldn't afford to be far away. If I was alone, if everyone on the ship was asleep....

A tremor rocked my body. Alone with Stephan? Alone with Mak?

I folded my hands in my lap, waited for the tremor to pass. Then I breathed myself slowly, deliberately into an artificial calm, let my eyes slid closed. Without Stephan my range was pitiful. Was it even worth the risk?

I opened my mind and reached.

Pain! God, so much pain!

I scrambled from the couch. I ran. I burst through the bedroom door, stumbled to a halt beside the bed. Cam lay sprawled across the mattress. Sleeping. Peacefully. Heart racing, head still reeling, I backed out of the room, pulled the door closed with a quiet click. I blew out a breath, pressed my forehead against the artificial wood. Tears of relief and fear stung at my eyes. I rubbed them away.

"Ashley, help me."

◆

I spun around to see Stephan stagger from the shadows near the apartment door. I blocked the entrance to Cam's room.

"You stay away from him."

Then I caught my breath as that incredible pain leaked from his brain into mine. I risked lowering my eyes from his and saw where he gripped his upper arm, saw his fingers covered in dark streaks in the monochrome night. Blood.

"He's got Ami, Ash."

Stephan dropped into a dining room chair, let his head drop back against the wall. His face clenched. I caught myself taking a step toward him, then stopped.

"He told me I've got fifteen minutes to get you and that fucking file back down to him or he's going to shoot her in the gut and fucking watch her bleed out." His whisper broke into a hiss through clenched teeth.

I turned around, reached for the door handle.

"Don't!"

I grabbed my head as his pain, his force of will invaded my mind. Stephan pushed off the chair and crossed the space between us. Gripping my arm, he dragged me toward the living room.

"Are you really trying to get her killed? Get the fucking file!"

A picture of Amilee cowering in the corner of some kind of garbage-filled storage closet, shaking and crying and begging flashed into my awareness. Stephan grabbing Mak's arm. The punch as Mak turns around and shoots him.

"God."

Shoving me toward the suitcase, Stephan sank onto the arm of the couch, his mental invasion slackening as the pain overtook him again.

Fear and anger. I couldn't work with that. I needed anger. Violent, vengeful anger. I thought of Jessie, Gerard, bleeding, suffering, lost. I thought of Cam and how there was no way I was letting that fucking psychopath touch him. I thought of Paula and her boy Brian, so innocent, vulnerable. And I thought of Amilee terrified and begging. The tremors in my hands slowed.

Act. Now.

I grabbed a pair of slacks and a suit jacket, pulled them on over my nightgown. I made a show of rifling through my bag, let him see me slide the twisted energy bar and the keycard into my pocket. Then I spun around, grabbed my workpad. With one hand I shut down the schematics file and yanked the stick. With my thumb, I set the pad's alarm at maximum volume.

I jogged over to the kitchen, left the workpad on the dining table, grabbed the towel from the refrigerator door. I slipped the stick in the tiny suit pocket at my breast. Something stabbed me in the finger. I hesitated.

A goddamn bug. Fuck! Yeah, they always found me. Was I a moron? They'd been tracking me.

Stephan snapped his head around. I erased the mortified realization from my head, from my face. He started to probe; I reached for his arm. He realized what I was doing and moved his hand. I tied the towel around the wound—for all the good it would do. I gave the knot a yank.

Stephan swayed. I grabbed his shirt; grabbed for his mind, yanked him back. He blinked at me but pushed to his feet.

"Where is she?" I demanded.

"Somewhere in the operations side. He was already moving her when I left."

"Fucking great."

I wrapped my arm around his waist and headed us toward the door.

◆

Both of us knew there was only one way we would find Mak and Amilee in time. Stephan could increase my range to nearly a quarter of the ship. If I let him in. Completely let him in.

I couldn't help but feel I'd been maneuvered into this position.

We cleared the vacant operations checkpoint. The gate had been pathetic as a deterrent. Back in with the lab rats. We made it to a windowed lounge area with laminate tables and metal chairs. I felt out with my limited range. All clear.

I released Stephan to the support of one of the tables.

I swore I wasn't going to start hyperventilating, but even I could hear the little screech in my breathing. I turned my head away and bit my lip. Hard.

Stephan started to raise his hand toward me. His blood soaked hand. He stopped. His intention stroked my cheek instead.

"I'm not going to hurt you, Ash."

I pressed my lips together, faced him.

"Just do it."

He laid his hands on my arms, looked into my eyes. My heart lurched.

"Relax."

I closed my eyes.

And opened to him.

He flowed into me, cool and liquid, so careful.

Time, time, we don't have time.

With a roar in my ears, he slammed into me, battering my brain and my body. The barriers of my mind blew apart, he filled me with endless waves of sensation—thoughts, images, emotions, so much fear, so much pain. I felt the edge of the table cutting into his thighs, the throbbing of his arm spreading its tendrils through his whole body. I saw myself with my head thrown back and thought I'd never seen anything so beautiful. He pulled me in and took my mouth, and I responded just as he'd remembered, just as he'd known I would.

Distantly, I knew I was drowning.

Amilee.

Stephan broke the kiss with a groan. A vague bubble of my consciousness bobbed to the surface.

"Which way?" he whispered, his lips still hovering over mine.

A vast, placid sea. Which way? No way. No way different from any other.

"Find Mak, Ash. Find Amilee."

Blinding rage. Snarling, lashing. I flinched away.

"That way, then," he muttered.

We walked. Endless white halls, rolling and pitching with the waves of contempt and anger getting stronger and stronger.

"Come on, Ash. I can't carry you. Talk to me."

Someone waded into my ocean.

"Oh, god, Ashley. Ashley, where are you!"

Here. For a while. And then not.

Something dug into me. Something yanked.

I gasped like a woman pulled from the deep. I clutched at Stephan, caught myself just before my knees buckled.

"Too much! It's not...like before."

Stephan grabbed my arm as I tried to right myself.

"We've only got three minutes left. Can you make it?"

I turned and pulled him, stumbling.

"This way."

In my ocean I could see them waiting: the guard, nervous and bored; Mak, pacing, tapping, spitting obscenities; Amilee, ripping the air with her terror, searching, always searching. In my vertigo, I reached for that shiny smooth wall, used it to guide me. But it moved, constantly bumping, jostling me.

Where were they?

I drew Stephan to a stop. We were going to run right into the guard. We didn't have to run right into the guard. Mak had tossed Amilee in a recycling chute. He thought it was just a garbage bin.

"This way."

I used my keycard on the door for the canister loading facility. The one I didn't know worked on this door when I'd used their recycling container so many days ago—because my boxes didn't fit down that recycling chute.

I led Stephan down the metal stairs, the traction stabbing into my bare feet.

"Hurry. He's heading toward her. Hurry."

I stumbled off the stairs. Stephan caught me, but I pushed his hand away.

"The recycling chute. Release the recycling chute."

Stephan ran ahead, despite the jarring to his arm that sent flashes of gray through our vision. He grabbed the lever and yanked. We heard the doors along the length of the chute slide open. We heard her scream. Stephan's terror looked at me, knew from me that she was still unharmed. I tried to pull myself together; I tried to hurry forward.

"He's coming. He's coming. Push—"

He understood. He propped his back against the giant wheeled bin. He saw me see her tumble, slide, hit. He shoved. Mak's bullets pelted the cardboard.

My legs finally locked in beneath me. I ran.

I hit the metal bin, toed my way up the side.

"Ami?"

"Ash? Oh, my god. Oh, my god."

"Give me your hand."

I got a wrist wrapped in fishnet. Mak's fury hit my too open mind. I dropped her. Almost dropped myself.

Control, control, control.

I waved a frantic hand at Stephan.

"Close—"

He saw what I saw, Mak trying to wedge himself into the chute. Stephan cranked the lever back, rammed it back into the closed locking position.

One more time I reached out for Amilee. This time we grabbed and heaved. She caught the lip and swung herself over. I lowered myself a little more slowly, a little more carefully.

I reached the floor, flung myself around, leaned back against the bin with my eyes closed. I felt like I was caught in a riptide, pulled out, slammed down again and again by the waves. I couldn't breathe. Thinking my own thoughts—spurts and jolts.

"Come on, Ashley."

I dug my hands into my hair, shook my head.

"It's not like before, Stephan. I can't. It's too much. It's everything!"

Amilee came back to me.

"Ashley, what?" But then she knew. She turned on him and I muffled a cry as her outrage, her hurt flooded into me. "You did your thing to her. You—"

"Did you want to be dead?"

"Undo it."

I opened my eyes. Stephan stalked back to us. His face was beginning to go gray from the pain and blood loss.

"Don't you get it? This is how it's supposed to be. There's one of her. There's one of me. We're supposed to be together. Like this."

Stephan grabbed my arm, tried to drag me forward. I twisted from his blood-smeared grip.

So, he reached for my mind.

I screamed.

That sound, that horrible sound of soul-deep death, ripped through the metal cavern, ricocheted, and shot back at us. Froze everything.

It's okay. It's okay, Ashley. I'm going to get us out of here. It's only until I can get you safe. You're going to be okay.

You have no right!

And then I lunged. The windows, the doors of his mind were mine. I gripped his will with my own and drove him back, ramming his wounded arm against a support beam. Then I dragged him back from the edge of consciousness.

"Get out. I helped you. This will be the last time. If I see you again, if I hear from you again, I will contact the law. I will confess to every last one of your burglaries. I will spend the rest of my life behind bars, if I have to, but I will not be controlled by you!"

Amilee stared at Stephan, then she turned to me.

"But Ash, Mak—"

I nodded.

"He's coming. You need to get out of here."

I looked at her pixie-bright face, bruised at the forehead, scraped at the cheek. I looked past her to Stephan's mystery-dark eyes in an ashen face. I memorized them as a tear slipped down my cheek...

"Go."

I reached into my tiny jacket pocket, pulled out the stick, palmed the bug. Amilee rose to her toes, gave me a hug and a little whisper.

"Chocolate pretzels and marshmallow crème."

I choked out a laugh.

Stephan stepped forward.

"At least this time I get to say goodbye."

I didn't answer, just leaned forward and hugged him on his good side, let him go.

"Go now. He's coming."

Of course. He was tracking me. But someone else was coming, too.

27

My head was still ripped open wide.

But I could focus, and I could think, and my legs stayed beneath me as I took the stairs two at a time back up to the door where we had entered. I stripped off the jacket and the slacks. Ran my nails quickly over the seams of the nightgown, but apparently, they hadn't been worried about locating me while I slept.

With the stick firmly in my grip, I unloaded my slacks of the keycard and that blessed mangled energy bar that so cleverly concealed my mini. Quickly, I preset the alarm to five seconds, the volume to deafening. Then I took off down the stairs.

◆

The guard was unarmed, but I wasn't leaving Cam and his people to face the gun in Mak's hand without at least some kind of warning.

Mak had found a supply closet near the loading facility's main door.

Can't find a fucking piece of solid metal in this goddamn fucking shithole?! Break that goddamn door off at the goddamn hinges! That bitch is dead. I'll fucking slaughter them. Fucking think they can leave...

My heart froze. I didn't want to hear his thoughts. I didn't want my mind so close to pure insanity. But I thought of Cam and the last time I'd seen him, sleeping so peacefully in those tousled sheets. And I kicked the clothes aside and eased the facility door open.

I set a chunk of wood from a pallet between the door and its frame. I gripped the mini in one hand and the stick in the other.

"Stephan..." Fear choked me for an eternal moment. At the sound of my voice, Mak leaned out the supply closet door. "Stephan said you were looking for this." My hand shook as I held up the stick. Those eyes. His intention grinned sickeningly.

He stepped out of the closet. I got a full visual of why he hated me so much. He saw Stephan fucking me, an image so vulgar, so debased it made my bile rise. Anything of Stephan's had to be his, had to be destroyed—and he could think of so many sick, sick ways it could be done.

I pressed my wrist to mouth, felt my lips gone cold. Mak took a step toward me.

"Stop." I jacked the stick into my mini. "Stay back or I fry it."

Mak pulled out his gun.

"Think you can push that button before I pull this trigger?"

"Yeah. I do. Lower the gun and I'll toss it to you. Shoot me and your billion-dollar black market share is gone."

God, I was going to lose it.

Mak lowered his gun.

Cam was close, so close.

Mak pulled out his knife. My whole body shook at the sight of that thing. I fell back an involuntary step and he laughed.

No more.

I pushed the alarm button and threw the mini at him, stick and all. The phone began to shriek, the unpadded hallway giving it an unearthly volume.

I dove back through the doorway, kicked the wood block free, and used all my weight to override the hydraulics. The first bullet hit the door.

I ran.

◆

No matter what I did, how far I climbed, I couldn't get far enough away from it. The terror, the pain, the screaming insanity—claws that ripped at my brain.

And then the dawn came.

And the two thousand people living aboard Pioneers' Port began to rise.

28

"Kaitlin. Kaitlin! I've found her. She's here in my apartment. Sharon, you gotta get up here. She's not... Oh, god, Sharon, hurry! I know. I know that. I didn't move her. I didn't touch her. Just get up here..."

◆

Light.

Trembling hands.

Fear. I rock with that fear on my endless ocean, calm it, soothe it. *It's alright. You're alright. Shh. Don't worry.*

"Kaitlin?"

◆

"Hey, Kaitlin, it's me, Gerard. They let me come up to talk to you. So...Uh, well, so Brian's going to be here in a couple days. Still haven't decided what to do with Paula and me, but they decided a boy ought to be with his mother. Probably not the best thing to tell you to convince you to come back, huh?

Hey, I'm sorry. You can be anybody you want to be, you can be the boardroom bitch. You can be the fucking damsel in distress. Just don't you leave me, too. Don't you fucking leave me."

◆

A warm body wraps around me, tries to hold me inside. But I'm sliding away, floating into darkness. I shouldn't be out here. I know what happens when you're out here.

Cam!

The warm body jerks away from me.

"Sharon, I'm losing her!"

◆

"This is Kaitlin, Brian. She's having a bit of a rough time."

"She gonna be okay?"

"I don't know, sweetie. We actually, we actually almost lost her last night. Do you mind if I talk to her for a minute? Here, you can take my workpad. Thanks, sweetie."

"So, I saw the video. They thought I might be able to tell them what was going on, might be able to figure out some way to help you. They keep looking for aneurisms and tumors—some kind of brain damage. It's not that, is it? It's your thing, your built-in intention detector. It got cranked up too high somehow, something to do with that guy. Oh. Oh, maybe...maybe... Brian, you stay right there."

29

A wet breeze played over my skin. The warm weight of filtered sunlight pressed down on me, so gentle and soothing. But the flesh of my left forearm swelled with a cold ache. I reached for it.

"Oh, my god. Kaitlin."

A hand gripped my upraised one. I opened my eyes.

Cam.

His appearance confused me. His face was tan, his hair sun-streaked. He was thinner, too, and carried an exhaustion that dampened the mysterious and beautiful light in his eyes. But the hard, cold snakes of torment and doubt had vanished. And in their place, something beautiful and warm and golden radiated, and it already filled me, my legs, my arms, my torso, my head—peace and joy and the profoundest relief.

I smiled at him, savored his smile in return.

I felt my eyelids lowering.

"So tired."

"I know. I'll be right here."

His fingers played through my hair as I drifted off to dreams.

◆

"It says here, that some of the first and best naturalist accounts of these islands were made way before Darwin got here. It says they were made by pirates and that you can sometimes still find Spanish doubloons washed up on shore."

I laughed. It had taken me three days, but I finally felt like consciousness was something I could hold onto. I rolled my head to the side in the deckchair that was my sick bed. He felt me watching, closed his book, and turned on his side to grin at me. That dance was back in his eyes. I could see the energy bouncing off him at the idea of pirates and lost treasure. I could see it, but I could still feel my own more tired humor. That was good. That was better.

"Maybe we could go look down on the beach for some old pirate booty."

Cam swung his legs around, jumped to his feet.

"Really?! You think you can make it?"

"Gotta start sometime."

His grin was huge and foolish, but his hands were strong and gentle as he helped me to stand and wrapped a sweater around me. Every day I thanked Jessie for keeping me fit and strong. My arms and legs were loose and unsteady, but I could feel already it would come back quickly thanks to his relentless regimen. However, for now, Cam and I wrapped our arms around each other's waists.

As I picked my way over loose shards and rolls of lava rock, he chattered happily about pirates and murder and cursed islands.

"Did you know they actually thought these islands moved? They call them the Enchanted Islands, but they meant they were cursed, because you'd finally make it here and there was nothing here to save you, no drinkable water, nothing! These really desperate guys would be sucking the juice out of cactus leaves just to stay alive.

"Oh, and the volcanoes," Cam paused long enough to pull me upright again when the piece of scrub brush I'd made a grab for didn't hold. "There was this seal hunting ship docked here one night when 'boom!' this volcano completely blows and its pouring all this steaming hot lava into the sea and these guys on the ship are like, 'oh, shit,' because they are on this wooden sailing ship and there's no wind and it's getting so hot that the guys are passing out. And then finally they feel this tiny breath of wind and they pop those sails up so fast, but even then they are floating past these rivers of lava and they know that if that tiny puff of wind dies, they're dead, too, but finally they glide out of this water that's almost at the boiling point and they can look back and watch the volcano that's like this amazing fireworks show. I wonder what that did to their ship. You think it sank after that because the wood got all twisted up?"

I was laughing so hard by this point, I couldn't see for the tears in my eyes. We'd made it down from our little encampment to the beach by this point. I turned into him as the sand poured into my sandals, reached up and pulled him down for a kiss.

He hummed against my lips.

"Do pirates get to kiss the pretty girls?"

I chuckled.

"I think they're more into rape and plunder."

Cam grinned and wiggled his eyebrows. I just shook my head. I stroked his tan, stubble-roughened cheek, drank in his giddy joy.

"This is good."

He nodded. "You're getting so much stronger, so fast."

"No, I mean you."

Cam's eyebrows shot up and he pulled back, so he could get a better look at me.

"Yes, you," I repeated. "You are so free, all the way to the core of your heart. You look so healthy, so happy. You never felt this way on the ship, not even on the first day I met you."

"Ha! Paula warned me that if I radiated anything but serenity and good cheer I would be yanked off this island so fast my head would spin. She wanted to send you out here alone. I told her I thought you could handle one person and it didn't take much to convince her that Dr. Sharon Smith had never radiated serenity and good cheer a day in her life.

"They say hello, by the way, her and Brian and Gerard, your two techs. Gerard's spending more and more time out of the wheelchair, kicking Brian's ass at Intergalactic Raiders."

I spotted a chunky boulder. Cam turned us a little and led us over to it. That gave me a little chill. It seemed...it seemed almost like he knew what I wanted the moment I wanted it. It made me pause, trying to remember how it had been in the beginning with Stephan and I, but I couldn't really remember. It didn't *feel* the same, though, no blank spots, no startled realizations that you'd done something you'd never intended to do. And so, I tried to find comfort in that.

We settled in and I tucked my head against his shoulder, pulled my sweater tight around me.

"I'm so glad to hear they're doing okay." I couldn't really bring myself to ask what was going to happen to them, or to me for that matter. Too much the coward. "Am I...am I allowed to ask about Mak?" Before I could catch it, a shiver ran through me that had nothing to do with the cool breeze of the ocean rolling over the sand before us. So much for my brave face.

"Only if it will keep you from worrying."

I stayed silent, waiting. Cam's intention wrapped around me, trying to protect me from my own fear.

"He's dead. He got a few shots off. Heather took one in the vest, but he was aiming for his own guy. And he got him. And then we got him."

"Heather okay?"

"Yeah, her vest's an antique, her dad's lucky vest from when he was on the force, so she's got a hell of a bruise, but hey, the vest is still damn lucky if you ask me."

"Yeah."

I raised my head a bit, looked around the empty sand.

"Isn't the Galapagos supposed to be famous for its gigantic tortoises?"

"I'm afraid on this island you're stuck with penguins."

"Penguins? On the equator?"

"Yeah, I thought I saw some down on those rocks the other day. Think you're up for it? Want to go take a look?"

I sat up straighter and turned to him.

"Right after you tell me what's bothering you."

"Ah," Cam pulled his hands away to rub them over his face. "I forgot it's impossible to keep secrets around you."

"You are the one who said you didn't 'do' secrets. Gave me a big lecture about pilgrims and the fate of nations resting squarely on the shoulders of Camden Glaswell."

"Ha! I have a feeling I will be changing my opinion on that one very soon."

"Spill."

"Ah, okay...you hugged them goodbye. You hugged *him* goodbye. And then you let them go."

Slowly, I nodded and as understanding bloomed in me, I saw the nauseated worry drain from his face. He was definitely reading me. I didn't know if he knew it yet, but he was definitely reading me. I pressed my lips together.

"Okay, how do I...? Okay, off with the band aid. They'd been tracking me. With bugs. These giant, completely hack..." I was blushing now. "Okay, so I'd finally figured that out after a whole week and I knew there was one in my jacket pocket. I palmed it and I planted it. But it's completely useless by now. I'm sure they're long gone." A realization that brought me both relief and unease.

Cam jumped up.

"That's why! The clothes by the door when we got in there. And why you were wearing that skimpy little nothing when I found you on the floor in my apartment." He whirled around on me with a warning finger. "And by the way, there is no one on the ship who doesn't know you and I have a thing now thanks to that outfit."

"A thing."

Cam's emotions stopped whirling like a little boy who'd hit the candy jar. He looked down at me. I ignored his intention as it stroked my face in favor of those gentle blue eyes. For a moment I was back in the restaurant on the ship, dreaming about flying off into the stars with him at my back, murmuring magic into my hair. He reached out for my hand.

I slid my fingers into his palm. I had never felt so fragile, so delicate. He pulled me to my feet, pulled me to him.

"More than a thing."

I shook my head. This was the part I didn't want to talk about, didn't want to think about. "When we get back to the ship—"

He put his finger to my lips.

"You—"

"I am not running. Not ever again. If I made choices that are seen as unforgivable mistakes in the eyes of the law, then...I'll just..."

The shaking snaked out from my stomach through my chest, out into my arms, out in my legs.

"Hey, shh, hey." Cam pulled me in tight. "You're not strong enough for this yet. Shh. Hey, let it go. Do I feel worried to you? Don't you think I'd be worried, if I thought Will was going to turn you over to the authorities? And no matter what, the Port doesn't fly a flag, but you're an American citizen. We're not just going to toss you in some dank, sweaty Ecuadorian jail cell to rot."

We.

My teeth started rattling in my head. Cam tilted my head back, made me look at him.

"Hey, look at me. Whatever Will and the captain decide, I'm going to be right there with you, okay? Okay? I'm not leaving you, alright?"

"'Kay."

I tried to smile for him. He raised an eyebrow at my pathetic attempt. His hands slid up my back, cupped my head. He sank his lips, softly, deeply into mine and then he kissed me and kissed me and kissed me and that might not have been enough, but his intention was never satisfied with just a kiss and soon my bones grew too loose and the tremors lost their grip.

Cam drew away, came back for one last taste, then pressed his forehead against mine.

"Now, I believe we came down here to check out some penguins."

"Doubloons. We're here for the treasure."

Cam unwrapped himself from around my body and started pulling me toward the rocks anyway.

"Speaking of treasure, you know there's legends about poor farmers on these islands pulling up stakes and leaving after sudden and mysterious 'improvements' in their fortunes. You never know, you might just get lucky."

I threw my head back and laughed. And as I listened to his excited chatter, I knew I was already so incredibly lucky and slipped my hand a little further into his and he held me tight.

30

Will told a story.

On the Mayflower there was a young man, an indentured servant by the name of John Howland. He'd become restless below and decided he had sea legs enough to withstand the winds and the waves of the furious sea above, so he climbed out on deck. He was wrong. The ship took a good hit and he was knocked over the railing and into raging waters. But strength, luck, and courage were on his side. He managed to catch a trailing rope and though he was plunged nearly ten feet under the waves with what must have been unimaginable force, his hand clung still to that rope when the sailors hauled him back onboard.

So, we sat before Will and Captain Le Roux: Paula clutching Brian's hand, Gerard with his cane, and me with my fingers over my shoulder laced in Cam's, and we must have truly looked pathetic because Will declared us the victims of accident and foolishness. He said that we had shown strength and courage through the dangerous results of our mistakes. Will told us that John Howland had gone on to become a leader in the colony

and the thirteenth signer of the Mayflower Compact. He
expected the same sort of full and meaningful lives of us.

Then, both he and the captain offered their condolences
and the captain departed. Will came around the table.

He crouched down in front of me, put his hand on my knee.

"If you ever get in that kind of trouble again, you come to
me. Or to Cam. Don't you hide it like that again. I'm not blaming
you. I know you did your best, but I trust you aren't the type
who needs to be thrown overboard twice."

"No, sir."

He patted my knee and rose, but his intention watched me
with concern as he moved on to Gerard. He thought I was on
the verge of losing it. Which was fair; I was. Cam gave my hand
a hard squeeze.

Will stopped in front of Gerard.

"I didn't realize it was you when Cam gave me the run down.
You're a lot skinnier than when I last saw you at your uncle's
house. I'll have to let him know you haven't managed to kill
yourself yet. Does the Senator even know you're out here?"

"Yes, sir."

Senator.

Cam gave my hand another squeeze. Yes, that senator. It
was Gerard, not Jessie who'd gotten me my new identity. I turned
my shocked gaze toward Gerard, but he was blocking me out
with the skill of years of long practice. I shook my head and left
him alone. For now.

Will stopped in front of Paula and Brian now.

"So, here's the big question: did I put payment down on a billion dollars of digital crap?"

Fire snapped through Paula's reserve, right into her eyes. "Our software is not crap. Even outside of testing mode, our software is fifteen percent more accurate than any other intention detection system out there."

"Then why the cheat, why the fraud?"

Paula shook her head, the fire washed away by loss, by tears.

"Because he, he said that if we could make the people under our care that much safer, even for the little while we were onsite, shouldn't we do that? Didn't we have the moral obligation to? He—" She wiped her eyes. "Sorry."

I had to look away. Gerard rubbed at his cheeks. I reached for his hand and he actually took it.

"Kaitlin's natural talent." That's what I had now. A *natural* talent. "You can't duplicate that with a computer. At least not yet. But he didn't want her to know. He thought it would mess her up. I always felt guilty about that part—the not telling her, but...but never about the rest."

That last part wasn't true. She felt guilty about all of it, but she would never say anything to smear Jessie's memory.

I felt the trembling start and had to close my eyes. I still couldn't handle a lot of emotion yet and this room was so full of sorrow and fear. Behind me Cam rubbed my shoulders.

"So, if she walked off this ship right now, I would still have the best hardware and software on the market?"

I opened my eyes. Paula cleared her throat, pulled Brian closer.

"Yes, sir."

"And Gerard, you can take over Jessie's portion of the contract obligations?"

Gerard looked up, looked startled for a minute.

"I would have to get up to speed. I have his reports. But the CEO stuff..."

"We can find somebody for that," I interjected.

"Good. Because tragedy or no, I still have a timeline with scheduled contracts on the other end of it. I need these systems in place by November."

I released Cam and Gerard and pushed to my feet. Will was satisfied with himself and feeling rather clever and smug besides. I intended to keep him that way.

"We'll have them ready, sir."

"Good. Then let's all get back to work."

SEVEN MONTHS LATER...

My mom is supposed to arrive today. I can feel her out there on that tender. I want to draw it nearer; I want to slow it down. She has a new husband I'll be meeting for the first time. I've never been so terrified in my entire life.

I'm not the Ashley she last knew. Like Jessie's artificial Kaitlin, that Ashley is gone from my head. I'm left with only myself to blame for any moments of crippling fear or brilliant bravado. Sometimes it's almost lonely in here. I'm so worried Mom won't recognize who I've become, that all these changes will be too much.

It's going to be fine.

I run my hands over the warm railing, see my finger glint in the sun. The diamond is a huge rectangle-cut mounted on a thin gold band. I run my thumb over the sharp edges. This is my space elevator, my gateway to a life that feels real and whole. The security project is finished, and Cam and I haven't decided whether we are staying on here or moving with Paula and Gerard and Cleo onto the project in Vegas. Maybe we'll try something new altogether.

I feel Cam walking up behind me. I turn my face up to the morning light as he pulls me in tight, rests his chin on my shoulder. The feel of his mind and body both soothes and inspires. We have so much ahead of us, so much to do, so much to try.

I hear the familiar rumbling hum of the platform rolling back.

"This one's the last practice run. The first real canister will start loading next week," he tells me.

Leaning my cheek against his soft hair, I smile. I've met some of the people who will be sleeping in that first canister. My runaways. Are they Wan Hu with his rocket chair? Are they righteous John Howard with his eyes on God? Are they Astronaut Stu Roosa ready to explore and to push the boundaries of human experience beyond this fragile little planet?

This canister is mostly Stu, but others are beginning to trickle in. And I can tell already who is ready, who is here for the reasons that will bring them through the struggle and who is not. Because everybody brings memories and regrets, joys and sorrows, but some people also packed themselves full of hope and full of the sure knowledge that they can become a part of something greater than themselves, something magical.

The elevator is above us now, rising, rising. And all the heads below are upturned, watching, hearts full of fear and wonder and excitement. And I wish them luck on their journey whenever, wherever it starts.

Because my journey begins right here, today.

Mom's tender has arrived.

Cam takes my hand and we head down the ramp to greet her.

AFTERWORD

The Story of Place: Capturing a place that won't hold still

When choosing a place whose story you are going to tell, it is usually easy: pick an interesting setting for your action and off you go.

Not so this time.

I thought I would be setting my story on the remains of the Kennedy Space Center: what a depthless treasure trove of tales that would be!

Here comes the sound of the brakes.

Apparently, the platform for a space elevator must be incredibly mobile. And in relatively calm waters. So actually, the best place for a platform is off the coast of the Galapagos Islands. Well, now there's a place with some pretty rich history. Sweet! A THOUSAND miles off the coast of the Galapagos. Damn!

So, there I sat with all this incredible research about the Apollo space program and its iconic astronauts. Pioneers into an impossibility, into the unknown. Pioneers. Pioneers. Pioneers...

And soon the "place" whose story I would tell became not a geographic location, but a place in life, a place in the heart and mind where—despite horrifying odds, daunting precedent, and dangers vividly imaginable—the dreamer nonetheless takes that step off the edge of safety and becomes the pioneer. Whether it's an astronaut, a Pilgrim, an explorer, a settler, or simply a woman who can no longer run away from her past, the decision must be made whether to stay in the supposed safety of their current lives or make that leap and maybe, just maybe achieve greater things than they ever thought possible.

The following are not my exclusive sources of legends and folk history by any means, but they are beautiful, inspiring books by every means, demonstrating the power of human courage and imagination:

Voices from the Moon: Apollo Astronauts Describe their Lunar Experiences by Andrew Chaikin with Victoria Kohl, designed by Daniel Lagin, published by the Penguin Group *(most of the quotes in the Breaking Free Observatory can be found here)*

Space Travel: A History by Wernher von Braun, Frederick I. Ordway, III, & Dave Dooling *(many of the stories in The Dream Observatory can be found here)*

Mayflower by Nathaniel Philbrick *(Will's favorite author)*

Galápagos: The Islands that Changed the World by Paul D. Stewart *(one of Cam's favorite guides to the islands)*

Liftport: Opening Space to Everyone edited by Bill Fawcett, Michael Laine, & Tom Nugent Jr. *(fact and fiction compiled by the people who made the first real push to turn space elevator technology into reality)*

May these books give you a glimpse of the past that inspires a future where:

"I have learned to use the word impossible with the greatest caution."

—Wernher von Braun,
    German Immigrant &
    Father of the American Space Program

1

People say you have to be suicidal to be in my line of work. Do I believe them? Depends on the day.

Some days being one of only six sensory immersion artists in the world means nothing more than listening. Like today. I listened to my naked feet complain about the lines of sharp cold pressing into them from the diamond-pattern catwalk; I listened to the tiny hairs on my legs, belly, arms, and face bask in the gentle flow of thick aquarium air...and I listened to my heart trip as the dark blue dorsal fin broke the water's surface in the isolation tank just a half meter below me.

Mo, my onboard AI recorded each of these sensations directly from my brain and sent them back to our library at Lone Pine Pictures.

This promised to be a hell of an enactment.

The only thing missing was the easy sibling-like banter I usually shared with the three other members of my team. Instead, we each occupied our own isolated section of the same two-meter strip of catwalk over the brightly lit isolation tank. The blame was mine. They didn't want to be here. I wasn't changing my mind.

End of discussion.

I gave Tamsin Leonides, our field producer and my best friend, the nod. The two aquarists and the marine biologist charged with the care of Ike, that juvenile blue shark pacing the water below me, had sensed the tension in my team. The biologist's thick, gloved fingers rapped on the railing, sending small vibrations through the bones of my elbows on the same hollow metal bar. I didn't want those boys going logical on me and balking.

Tamsin wandered casually in their direction.

I knew what the three men were thinking: Ike was a national treasure, rescued from the toxic soup formerly known as the Atlantic Ocean. I was a billion-dollar piece of movie-making equipment. The orderly parts of their scientific minds would see the combination and extrapolate the most likely outcome—a very public disaster and the end of their distinguished careers.

Fortunately for the livelihood of my team, Tamsin was the most innocent of con artists. She easily pinned the trio on the ladder platform. Out of the corner of my eye, I watched her block their mental retreat with an arsenal that was one part professionalism, one part enthusiasm, and two parts well-built, blue-eyed blonde. People tell me I'm intimidating. Not Tamsin. She's approachably pretty. Then she opens her mouth and people fall in love.

"Oh, no, not at all. She's brilliant with animals. In all the years we've been doing this, we've never had a serious animal accident. In fact, you should have been there, Jessie. You would have loved it. You remember *Spirit Guide*, that wolf movie? Well, when we were doing the enactment for that scene where..."

Behind me I heard Ben Norris-Stevenson, our stunt coordinator and my bodyguard, make a choking sound barely audible above the filtration system. Even I cracked a smile. I suppose Tamsin's claim depended on your definition of "serious." Possibly your average urbanized citizen would consider having her tibia cracked by grizzly bear fangs "serious." Or maybe getting a few ribs shattered by a pissed off buffalo would fit the bill.

But Tamsin's little exaggeration was safe. When the shark boys looked over at me, all they saw were long expanses of unmarred skin courtesy of my onboard medic, Margie. Gotta love Margie.

Satisfied that the progress of the enactment was in good hands, I squatted down next to Ryan Gunner, our swarm operator. It was time to integrate with the swarm cameras and get this show on the road.

Even in a crouch Ryan was at least a head shorter than me with sleek short brown hair, a slightly Hispanic cast to his features—as opposed to my hint of the Orient—and a timeless baby face he had finally stopped trying to hide with that ridiculous beard. He gave me one quick glance and then kept his gaze studiously averted. It wasn't because he had issues with the bikini, either. He'd seen me in less.

Grief makes some people uncomfortable. My way of dealing with grief—with this off-schedule enactment—made my people *very* uncomfortable.

I watched him work for a minute as he dragged icons across the clipboard, logging a selection of cameras into the library I use to create sensory tracks for Lone Pine's full-immersion films. It wasn't my way to play other people's games. The awkward silence was theirs, not mine. I didn't feel the need to honor it.

Especially when there were things I genuinely wanted to know.

"How was Haylee? Did she like that Rumpelstiltskin book?"

"Yeah, it was a good pick. Monitor showed all kinds of spikes. So, um, thanks for letting me take the detour."

Haylee is Ryan's six-year-old niece. She's six years old today. She was six years old ten years ago. Haylee is one of the victims of Sleeper's Syndrome, a disease that put thousands of kids sixteen and under into a stasis-like coma. She "sleeps" in the Children's Castle down in Vermont.

Haylee was the sweet, sad reason Tamsin and I picked the aquarium in Portland, Maine, instead of something a little closer to Montana where we're based.

"I'm sorry I wasn't able go with you this time," I murmured.

Ryan still wasn't meeting my gaze, but his fingers stopped sliding over the camera settings on his clipboard. "No big deal. You had your own stuff to deal with."

I just nodded. The conversation was started. That was good enough. I reached past him and pulled the sheet of camera focus dots from his gear box.

"How many?" I asked.

"Nine little water birds." Ryan finally looked up at me, his soft eyes wary. I could see him gathering up his courage to cross the line. He wasn't heeding my mental "no." Maybe I needed to work harder on my telepathy.

"But, Alyse—"

I stood up and turned away. Not enough to say "fuck off," just enough to say "not now." Ryan wasn't a personal issues kind of guy. He dropped it.

So instead I got Ben.

Great.

How hard could it be to understand I just needed to get this over with?

Ben stepped forward from the rail, his normally cheerful face grim. I shot him a pointed look. I wasn't going to break my concentration by talking about why I was here or even thinking about it. My heart was already beginning to race despite the calm concentration I'd spent the last hour building up. My eyes strayed to the shadow image of the predator drifting around the edges of the small pool below us.

Ben reached out his hand. I turned over the sheet of focus dots. His elegant black fingers precisely placed the first dot between my eyebrows, applying an even pressure without brushing my skin. Ben respected how much I hated being touched skin to skin. If only he respected how much I was done talking about this.

"Alyse, we're here for you, baby, but—"

"Ben," I warned. Subtle body language did not work with this man.

The only member of our team taller than me, he stared me down for a long moment. For such a goofy guy, he could do intimidating really well with that bald head, trim moustache and goatee, and chiseled face. Unfortunately for both of us, I was used to it. Finally, he let his hand drop.

"Alright. What do you look for?" he asked, peeling off the next transparent dot and pressing it between my breasts. He let his gaze linger on what my tiny pale blue bikini top revealed before he moved on to my shoulders.

That's Ben for you. The prince of subtlety.

"Arched back, cocked tail, lowered pectoral fins, shaking head...Ben, he's barely a meter long. He's just a baby."

"Alyse, that baby got teeth on its *skin* can rip you open. Forget about the ones in its mouth."

"We've done worse."

"Yeah, but not when your head was cut off from your common sense."

Behind Ben, I saw Ryan jerk his gaze away. I carefully breathed out my retort. I wasn't going to let them rattle me. That wasn't something I could afford during an enactment. Not only did it taint the sensory data, but most predators had built-in fear detectors and I had no wish to introduce myself as potential prey.

One dot went between my shoulder blades. Then Ben hooked my bikini bottoms with his pinky finger and tugged them down a centimeter. His knuckle accidentally brushed my spine. I shuddered.

"Sorry."

"Trying to make Steffi jealous?"

"Not if I want this dick the same length when I wake up tomorrow morning."

Ben gave me a second to settle out before he placed one dot just above my tailbone and one just below my navel. I pulled my rice-stick-straight black hair into a knot and he attached a dot to the crown of my head and one to the sole of each foot. Despite his best efforts, by the time he was done, my whole body was humming. And not in a good way.

I stretched, then let my muscles fall loose, shook it off as best as I could.

"This is going to be a beautiful enactment, Ben. Make you millions of dollars. Now stop wringing your hands like an old lady and let's get to work."

Ben stepped back. "Look at me," he demanded. I obliged, if just to get it over with. "Me and Steffi are still expecting you to come out to the track with us on Friday. You fuck up here and miss that, Steffi's gonna kill me. She's got Monique all greased up and ready for you."

Another retort to choke on. Steffi hates me and I'm not sure I feel much better about her.

But I appreciated his intent and valued his friendship even more. Okay, and maybe I really liked gunning Monique, his vintage 1998 Corvette convertible, through the defensive driving course at the Kalispell Antique Auto Course. You caught me.

"Understood." I gave him my warmest smile while he stood there with his arms weirdly at his sides. It frustrates Ben to no end that I don't do hugs—like he has something important to say, but somebody cut out his tongue. Finally, he brushed a hand over my hair and finally, finally let it drop.

It was time.

Steady, so steady, I turned back to Ryan. "Think we're ready to get started here."

Ryan opened the case and released the swarm. Each tiny camera rose into the air about a half a meter away from my body and fixed on its target dot. It used to distract me the way each video-camouflaged little globe would mimic my every move, zipping in and out, dodging obstacles, but always staying in line with its focus dot on my body. After nine years I rarely noticed it any more.

What I did notice was the little blue fin, and the smaller tail that followed it, still drawing rippled V's in the water beneath my feet. I knelt down and peered out between the blue horizontal bars of the railing. Ike rose close to the surface. He peered back up at me with his flat dark eye. Black to black our gazes held.

My dad had been a volunteer nature reserve keeper in Fiji. He used to tell a story about the shark god Dakuwaqa. He said that the shark god lost a fight against the octopus god that guards the island of Kadavu and, to save his own life, Dakuwaqa promised never to harm anyone from Kadavu whenever they went out to fish or to swim.

I reached my hand out over the water. The young shark seemed to hover. My heart, my soul hovered with him.

My dad, he *wasn't* from Kadavu....

TONYA MACALINO

lives in that space Between—where the crossroads of past and present tease the senses, taunts the almost-memory. Haunted by story, she seeks it in the shadows of the landscapes of history and in the blinding glare of what-may-come, both alone and with her family of children's book authors: Raymond, Damien, & Heléna Macalino.

For adults, Tonya's national award-winning supernatural thrillers, THE SPECTRE OF INTENTION and THE SHADES OF VENICE series, combine the mythic surrealism of Pan's Labyrinth with the thrill ride that is Lara Croft: Tomb Raider.

For children, Tonya's highly acclaimed urban fantasy adventures, THE GATES OF AURONA series, remind readers of the magical family secrets from Spiderwick Chronicles as well the legendary call to heroism of Chronicles of Narnia and the Dark Is Rising.

Need another glimpse behind the veil? Subscribe to Tonya's Reader Group at www.tonyamacalino.com for free books, guides, videos, and more! You can also drop by and chat with her on Facebook at www.facebook.com/TonyaMacalino.

Made in the USA
Monee, IL
31 July 2021